# HOPE CONTINUALLY

# HOPE CONTINUALLY

*by*
Dana Pride

Everlasting Publishing
Yakima, Washington
USA

# Hope Continually

*by*
*Dana Pride*

*ISBN: 0-9852739-8-4*

*ISBN-13: 978-0-9852739-8-9*

First Edition
Everlasting Publishing
P.O. Box 1061
Yakima, WA 98907

Dedicated to my husband,
true inspiration, and to
pastors everywhere.

# HOPE CONTINUALLY

*"But I will hope continually, and will yet praise thee more and more."*

*Psalm 71:14*

*King James Version (KJV)*

## NOW

Shannon Stronghart walked ahead of her husband and the police officer, dreading each step as it brought her closer to the back door of the church. The wind was biting and the air was nippy. A shiver made her entire body shudder as she fumbled for her keys. Her hands felt fat and slow, not wanting to open the door, reluctant to show the inside of the building.

In the darkness, she struggled to see which key fit the back door lock. She silently cursed the city for not replacing the light bulb in the streetlight.

"Come on, get that door open," the officer growled, "and I mean, NOW."

His stern voice made her jump. She finally forced the key into the lock, lifted and twisted while holding the door knob, the only way to get the key to turn in its rusty old mechanism. The door was damp and heavy on its hinges, protesting as she pulled on it.

The inside of the building was not any warmer than the outside, but at least she couldn't feel the wind in here. Her mind was spinning as she was shivering. What was he expecting to find here? They were in a poor neighborhood and the church building had nothing of value to the outside world. She switched on the light in the kitchen and turned to face the two men.

"This is it, *Pastor*," the officer sneered, leaning into her husband. "Your jig is up."

## BEFORE

### Harold

Harold Trumbuck sat on the edge of his bed, defeated. He was at the end of his rope. He had no hope, nothing left to live for. He was never going to get a date and now even his boss was snubbing him. Why had he been passed over for the promotion? He always worked much harder than Gregory Snotzer, who was late for work half the time and left early three-quarters of the time. Just because Snotzer had the good kind of hair and was always kissing up, the boss liked him better than he liked Harold.

His apartment was gloomy and cold. This morning his car had refused to start, so he had ridden the city bus to work, among the homeless, the losers and the mentally ill who rode around town all day with nothing to do. That's probably why his boss had decided to not promote him – he had lumped Harold in with the other losers.

That's what he was: a loser. He had nothing worth anything in his life, and now was the time to end it. The world would be better off without a loser like him, and he would be better off anywhere else but here.

He looked at the gun in his hand, turning it over, but not really seeing it. This was his ticket out of here. He would make sure it was loaded, then he would simply put it in his mouth and pull the trigger. He wouldn't think about the taste; he wouldn't have enough time for that. He would just open his mouth, and boom! It would all be over.

## Patricia

Patricia Addison slowly opened her eyes and squinted against the brightness of the morning. Where was she? What time was it? What day was it? As she tried to move, she felt the crushing of her head as it exploded and imploded at the same time. Wait – where were her kids? Did she leave them with someone? She really had to pull herself together. She needed to get high so she could think straight.

She looked around the bare room. She had been sleeping on a floor with a shoe for her pillow. There was no bed, no chair, no rug, no table, nothing. She didn't have the strength to lift her head, much less, sit up. If she could just get another hit, she would have the motivation she needed to get started with whatever she had to do today.

Or maybe she didn't have to do anything today. Wasn't that why she was here, in this strange place, all alone? Kandy and Lesly and Lonny – yes, those were their names, she had birthed them and she could recall their names – were somewhere else and they were in good hands. She didn't have to worry about them. All she needed to do was to get another hit, just a little one, so she could go on with her life. Things would come together however they would come together and they were out of her hands. Maybe after her nap, she could go somewhere, but now, with this crushing headache and no pain relief in sight, she had to go back to sleep. Her eyelids were heavy and her eyes didn't want to focus. She let her head roll to the side as she slipped back into darkness, easy numbness.

## Chester

Chester Deacon awakened his wife, Sandra, early on Sunday morning. Sunday was his favorite day of the week. He loved taking his wife to church. He gave her a quick kiss on the cheek and jumped into the shower. He had a feeling this was going to be a great day, and he wanted to savor every moment of it. He felt like singing praises to God, but he didn't know how to sing and he couldn't remember the words to any songs.

As he stepped out of the shower, he smelled the bacon cooking. Sandra always fixed a nice, hearty breakfast for them, even though they also went to have breakfast at their pastor's house every Sunday. His stomach growled loudly.

"Are you ready for breakfast?" Sandra called from the kitchen.

"I am on my way!" he yelled from the bedroom. He put on the church clothes she had set out on the bed for him and walked joyfully to the kitchen.

"You are in a great mood today," Sandra said, as she served his breakfast.

"This is the day the Lord has made," Chester replied, eyeing the bacon, eggs and toast on his plate. "I will rejoice and be glad in it."

"That is the Scripture," Sandra said, smiling, "but I don't know how you can be so happy when Linda and Brenda both have the flu."

"They are going to get over the flu," Chester said, lovingly embracing his wife. She always worried too much about her sisters. "Why don't you say a prayer for the food and then you will feel better."

"Saying a prayer isn't going to make Linda and Brenda feel any better," Sandra protested.

Chester smiled to himself as he saw his wife pouting. She could really be over dramatic, and he loved her just the same.

"Saying a prayer will make us feel better," Chester said, "and then we can eat, and then we will really feel better. Come on, we don't want to be late to Pastor's house."

## Pastor Stronghart

Pastor Stronghart reviewed his notes for his sermon. His schedule was so full, he had to do his daily Bible study and sermon preparation before the sun came up. Even on Sundays, his phone would ring four or five times before breakfast, so he needed to finish his study time early in the morning. He wasn't uneasy or irritated about this; it was all part of ministry, and he loved ministry.

He prayed over his sermon notes as he stuck them in his Bible. He glanced at the clock. He would have just enough time to take a shower and get dressed before their regular Sunday breakfast visitors arrived.

As he made his way up the stairs, he smelled the bacon and his stomach rumbled. He was really hungry, but he couldn't eat much on Sunday mornings before preaching a sermon.

"Something smells good!" he called to his wife.

"Yes, thank you," she said, stepping out of the kitchen to give him a kiss. "Everything will be ready just about the time Brother Chester and Sister Sandra get here." She returned to the kitchen, where she was grating potatoes to make hash browns.

"Are the kids stirring yet?" he asked. "We need to be on time today."

"They are both getting dressed," she answered.

"Good. I'm going to hop in the shower."

The phone rang. He glanced toward it, then remembered that he was on a time schedule. Answering the phone right now could make them all late for church, if it were one of the members calling him with a long, drawn-out problem and explanation of why he couldn't come to church today.

"Take a message for me," he said, as he went down the hallway.

## Shannon

Shannon set the table with napkins, silverware and glasses, and was preparing to fry the eggs when the doorbell rang.

"Zooey, can you get the door? Or Ethan?" she called out to her children. Zooey was thirteen years old; Ethan was about to turn nine.

Neither one answered her, the front door opened, and Brother and Sister Deacon came tumbling into the house.

"Hey-hey-hey!" Chester yelled, his voice booming. "This is the day the Lord has made!"

"Baaaaaaad news," Sandra groaned, in a way only she could groan.

"Good morning," Shannon said cheerfully. She had learned she could not get caught up into the fluctuating moods of others. She needed to push the positive attitude, all the time, or she would be as up and down as the people she came in contact with.

"But Linda and Brenda are both sick," Sandra moaned. "I think it is something really serious and they both have it. Linda started coughing on Tuesday and Brenda had a sore throat on Wednesday. They will probably both end up in the hospital, and then what are we going to do?"

"Hospital?" Shannon asked, shaking her head. "Nobody is going to the hospital. Probably by the time we get home from church, you will have the great news that they are both feeling much better."

"Yes, Dear, by the time we get home from church,

we will have great news that they are both feeling a lot better," Chester told his wife encouragingly.

"You could be right," Sandra said, somewhat encouraged.

"Of course they are right," Pastor Stronghart said, sweeping into the room with a big hug for Chester and Sandra.

"But Linda and Brenda –" Sandra began.

"I know, I heard, and they are both going to be feeling much better," Pastor Stronghart said with confidence. "And we don't have to wait until after church. Watch this." He threw both of his hands in the air and waved them in the direction where Sandra's two sisters lived. "Father, in the name of Jesus, we ask RIGHT NOW that You touch these two sisters with Your healing touch! We have seen You move like this before, and we are believing and expecting You to move again, RIGHT NOW! Touch them, Lord! And we give You all the praise, honor and glory, in the precious name of Jesus. Amen."

"Amen," Chester, Sandra and Shannon repeated.

"I would call them and ask if they are feeling better, but they are probably both still asleep," Sandra said, as she settled into her place at the table.

"You don't have to call them now," Pastor Stronghart said, "because God is already moving."

"Hi, Sister Sandra and Brother Chester," Zooey said cheerfully, as she came into the kitchen.

"Good morning, my little Sweetheart," Sandra said, her mood having been flipped a hundred eighty degrees. She stood up to close herself around the teenage girl, and her husband wrapped his arms around both of them. "Group hug!"

"I want a group hug!" Ethan said, as he popped into the kitchen and joined them. They all hugged for a moment.

"Did you get a new tie?" Sandra asked Ethan, looking him up and down.

"No," Ethan said, shaking his head and sitting at his place at the table.

"Ethan, take off your tie until after we eat," Shannon said.

"Can I help you, Mom?" Zooey asked, stepping over near her mother.

"You can pour the orange juice," Shannon said, as she broke an egg into the frying pan.

"Yummm, it sure smells good!" Sandra said.

"Did you make biscuits?" Chester asked.

"No, we are having fried eggs and bacon with hash browns and toast," Shannon replied.

"Home made hash browns!" Sandra exclaimed when she saw the frying pan. She again settled into her seat.

"We know how much you love them," Pastor Stronghart said.

Everyone sat in their regular seats and Zooey poured juice in small glasses. Shannon brought the eggs from the stove and placed them on the plates.

"These eggs are perfect!" Zooey said, as she watched the steam rise from them.

"Let us pray," Pastor Stronghart said. "Brother Chester, can you bless the food?"

They all joined hands as Chester said a prayer. When he was finished, they began to eat heartily. Shannon was pleased as she watched the group enjoying the food she had prepared. She had only fixed herself a small amount, because she needed to finish getting ready for church. As she stood up from the table, the phone rang.

"Do you want to answer it?" Pastor Stronghart asked. "You can let it go to the message machine. We don't want to be late to church."

Shannon glanced at the caller ID before deciding to pick up the receiver. "Good morning… yes… praise God! Yes, they are here and we all said a prayer for you, just a few minutes ago, and now we know God has answered our prayer! Okay, I'll tell her. Love you, Sister Brenda."

"That was Brenda?" Sandra asked, her eyes widening. A smile spread across her face, with child-like amazement.

"Praise God, she is feeling much better! And so is Linda!" Shannon said. "Brenda said she just woke up a couple of minutes ago, and she doesn't feel sick at all!"

"Hallelujah to the Lord!" Chester shouted, waving his hands in the air.

"What a mighty God we serve," Pastor Stronghart said.

"He always answers our prayers," Zooey stated matter-of-factly, as she spread strawberry jam on her toast.

## Officer Shotgun

Officer Ted Shotgun slowed his vehicle as he passed the old, weathered church on his route. This was a terrible neighborhood, filled with drunks, addicts, pushers and whores. The small parking lot was full today, and the nice cars sitting there seemed oddly out of place. The only people who had cars like that in this neighborhood were dealers.

He made a U-turn and pulled his car to a stop in front of the church. He could feel a pounding, a vibration, so he let his window down. It sounded like several hundred people were inside that little building, shouting, yelling – what were they doing? They had to be doing something illegal in there.

He glanced again at the row of nearly new cars in the parking lot. His nose for trouble was telling him that something was stinking here. Something was going on inside that church and he was going to find out exactly what it was. They had to be doing something illegal in there to lure people from other neighborhoods into this ghetto area. He started to get out of his car. Anyone could go into a church, right? Even him.

A call on his radio pulled him away from his present interest – for now – but this was not the end of it. He would be back, he would catch these criminals in the act of whatever it was they were doing, and he would shut down this operation. He would make it his top priority.

## Pastor Stronghart

"Since our church clerk is not here, Sister Stronghart will read the announcements today," Pastor Stronghart said from the pulpit, then he continued, "but first, let's have a Bible count. How many of you brought your Bible this morning? Hold up your Bible. Let me see it." He stopped and looked over the congregation, noting that some people even had two Bibles with them, the regular Bible as well as a purse or pocket edition. "Praise God, it looks like everyone brought your Bible today! Thank you. You can put them down now.

"You know, Ephesians 6:17 tells us that the Bible is the sword of the Spirit, and the book of Proverbs tells us that this book contains wisdom, but we have to dig for it. Wisdom is a hidden treasure, like a treasure chest, inside the Word of God, and the Holy Spirit is the key that unlocks that chest and reveals wisdom to us. But wisdom is not for the lazy person to find, much like gold. In the 1800s, the gold miners did not just find gold by staying home, nor was gold laying there all over the desert. The miners had to search for it and dig for it, diligently, before they could find it. It's the same way with the Word of God. We have to dig deep into it, study it diligently, and ask the Holy Spirit to give us that wisdom.

"Do you see your Bible as a treasure chest, or does it sit on the shelf all week until Sunday, when you dust it off and bring it to church? I was at a family's home, and their mother had passed away, so they asked me to come and minister to the family at home. When I got there, I asked if they had a Bible, so I could give them some verses, some comfort from the Word of God, if you will. Do you know, it took them about ten minutes to find their Bible, and when they finally brought it to me, it was completely covered with dust! It probably had not been used in years.

"I am encouraged today that you all have your Bibles, and some even have two with you today. You should always have your Sword handy, because you never know when God will put you in a situation where you will need it. Thank you."

He turned to his wife, who was waiting in her seat. "Sister Stronghart, can you come up and do the announcements at this time?"

His wife gathered some papers and stepped up to the podium. Pastor Stronghart silently prayed for each person in the sanctuary, and every family represented by these few people. Each family here had issues, problems that only the Lord could solve. A pastor could give advice, he could visit the sick, he could point people in the direction to where they could get financial assistance, but only God could make a real change in their lives. So many of them were under generational curses, the children repeating the sins of their parents and grandparents, with no other path before them. The pastor's job was to point people to Christ, the One who would give them a new path to follow, with hope and a new attitude to go with it, along with the staying power of the Holy Spirit they would need to stay on that new path. Most adults only saw the smudges in their own lives and especially the mistakes in the lives of others, but God could see each person's potential to do great things and to live a victorious life. Pastor Stronghart constantly prayed that God would give him eyes to see the great potential inside His people, as well as the guidance to point them to their triumphant destinies. He would preach this morning as if to a full congregation, as he did every Sunday.

## Shannon

Shannon stood before the congregation, reading the announcements of the upcoming church activities for the week. She tried to not think about how few people were here today, to not focus on the fact that they had 542 people on the church membership roll and fewer than twenty people in the service today. She often thought about and prayed for the hundreds of members who didn't regularly come to church – rotating in and out about a hundred of them – but today she focused on the members who had made the effort to come to Sunday morning service. The ones who were here today were not asking for a handout or trying to see what they could get from God or from their pastor. They were here to worship. She could tell by the joy on their faces as they looked at her attentively, as she read the weekly schedule. Most of these members would be participating in the Sunday evening service, Tuesday Bible Studies, Wednesday Noon Prayer, Thursday Choir Rehearsal, and early next Sunday for the Sunday School class. Shannon had learned from her husband long ago to concentrate on the Lord and what He was doing, not on what people were doing or not doing. In the twenty-seven years that she had been a member of this church, she had seen a complete exchange of members more than once.

As she looked at this Sunday morning group, the regulars of the past few years, she didn't see one person who had been with them since the beginning, when her husband had founded this church. Brother Chester and Sister Sandra Deacon had been faithful members since they had joined about eleven years ago, only missing two Sundays in all those years, when they had gone out of town on vacation. Sandra's other sister, Sister Tammy, was married to the assistant pastor, Pastor Fields, and they had been coming to Total Missionary Baptist Church for nearly fifteen years. Brother Jason, twenty-five years old and on fire for God, had been baptized about a year ago and he had not missed a Sunday since then; plus he had brought his three friends, Matthew, Paul and Chris, part of a younger crowd who were excited about the ministry and regular in their attendance.

Brother Lorenzo and his girlfriend, Sister Conya, had joined the church a few months ago, along with their little girl, Ebony, who was seven years old, and the older mothers of the church, Mother Bernetta and Mother Judith, were sitting in their regular seats in the front row on the left side of the room, with Zooey and Ethan behind them. In the back row were Sister Jane and Sister Barbara, both very quiet, nice middle-aged women. Mother Lessie sat in her wheelchair at the side of the front pew with joy glowing on her face. The congregation was a nice mix of an interracial crowd, a group that wouldn't be expected to be together in any other type of situation.

"Also, the TV Ministry schedule for this week is listed in your bulletin," she said, as she finished reading the weekly schedule, "and we will be recording again next Sunday.

"Please see Pastor Stronghart if you feel that God is leading you to volunteer for one of our other ministries: the Hospital Ministry, Jail Ministry, Nursing Home Ministry, Food Bank Ministry, Homeless Shelter Ministry,

Neighborhood Evangelism or Street Ministry, downtown. God has something for everyone to do."

"Don't be shy about the gift God has given you," Pastor Stronghart added. "So many people tell me they don't have anything to do for the Lord, but we have opportunities for everyone, right here at Total Missionary Baptist Church. This is one reason we are called Total Missionary, because we minister to the total person, and we are a missionary church, going out – not to other countries, but right here, in our own town – to minister to those who are in need. Everyone needs the love of Jesus, and the only way some people are going to know Him is through us. Please, see me if you are interested in any of these areas of ministry."

## Carolina

Carolina looked around her apartment with a sigh of despair. The place was in such a mess, but who else would see it besides her? She felt so tired, so heavy, so listless. She hadn't spoken with anyone in days, and she didn't have the energy to even find her phone. Her daughter, Patricia, had not spoken with her in three years. Carolina was worried about Patricia, but what could she do to help her daughter? At this point, she couldn't even much help herself.

She glanced across the room at the newspaper. Wasn't that the paper she had put in the garbage a few days ago? How could it be on the coffee table again? She summoned her strength and pulled herself out of her recliner. She really needed to lose some weight. She had stopped stepping on her scale when it showed she was over its limit of 299 pounds, and she certainly was not about to go to a doctor to get on one of those industrial scales. No, she just had to force her will power to keep her from over eating. But at this moment, her goal was to get that newspaper and put it in the trash – again.

She stepped over garbage and magazines, steadying herself by holding onto furniture until she finally grabbed that newspaper. She now needed to rest before she could go into the kitchen and toss it in the trash can. She flopped into the nearest chair to catch her breath. Her eyes fell upon a color photo on the front page of this section, a photo of a woman with her hands on the forehead of a man. They both had their eyes closed, and another woman and a little girl in the background also had their eyes closed.

Carolina read the caption: "Evangelist Margaret Dillon prays for Pastor Stronghart at Total Missionary Baptist Church." What foolishness! What a waste of time! If those people were Christians, they should be out helping other people, not just standing in a church and praying. Carolina crumpled up the newspaper and struggled to stand again. She found her cane propped up by the end of the sofa and used it to help her get into the kitchen. Good-bye, ridiculous article in last week's newspaper!

She was now too tired to walk all the way to her bedroom for a nap, so she collapsed again into her recliner. Before her eyes could make it all around the mess of a room, she had dozed off, promising herself that she would do better later, both on her diet and taking care of her apartment.

## Harold

Harold turned the gun over in his hand, again and again. He had never noticed how shiny it was, how heavy it felt as he passed it from one hand to the other. He was going to take care of his business today. He didn't need anyone and nobody needed him. He could almost feel himself slowly spinning, going down the drain of a cesspool. Negative thoughts were compounding in his mind; every phrase began with 'no one' or 'never' or 'nothing.' No one cared. Nothing mattered. Never had anything positive happened in his life. Nothing was worth living for.

His room was so silent, he could hear a ringing in his ears. Well, his neighbors would soon be hearing something more than a ringing. He had never fired a gun – this one had been his father's and Harold had kept it locked up ever since his father had died eight years ago – but he knew guns made a very loud sound. The silence seemed to be growing deafening; he had to have some kind of noise in the room so he could concentrate on this one last task and get it over with, and get his joke of a life over with. He reached for the remote to his TV with his left hand, still holding the gun in his right, and pushed the button to turn on the TV. Any sound would be better than this ringing in his head, which he would be stopping in just a few seconds.

"You might feel like life is not worth living," the voice from the TV boomed.

Harold looked up, startled. His heart skipped a beat. The man on TV was looking straight at him, a black man, one of those TV preachers.

"You might be contemplating suicide," the preacher continued, his voice softening, filling with kindness.

"So, what if I am?" Harold challenged. His heart began to pound. How could this guy possibly know?

"Suicide won't solve your problems. Only God can solve your problems. He knows all about them, and He cares," the preacher said compassionately.

Harold felt tears of sorrow welling up in his eyes, the first emotion he had felt besides anger in a long time. Could it be true that God did care about him?

"If you are out there, watching right now, and you feel separated from God, this is your day. You can come to Jesus just as you are. No matter what your problem might be, He has the answer. He can help you. He wants you to ask Him for His help, whatever your situation may be. Nothing is too hard for God. Take your burdens to the Lord and leave them there. He is waiting for you."

Harold set the gun on the dresser beside the TV. He began to feel something else he hadn't felt in such a long time – a smidgen of hope. He had shut the door to the possibility that things could get better for him, but now he felt, just maybe, they could.

"I want to pray for you, where ever you are, whoever you are, listening to me and watching me right now."

Harold knew this man was talking directly to him. The only way that could be possible would be if God were speaking through him. God must have wanted Harold to stay alive for some reason.

"God has great plans for you," the preacher was

saying, his voice growing louder. "He hasn't brought you this far to leave you now. He still has something for you to do.

"Father, in the name of Jesus, I ask that You touch that person who was, until few moments ago, contemplating suicide, and take away that idea of self-harm. Replace it, Father, with Your love, Your love that can and does change things, Your love that can change hearts, Your love that can work miracles and heal hidden injuries. Father, I ask that You move in the life of this person right now and relieve his burdens. Father, give him peace, the peace that passes all understanding, and, Father, I ask that You draw this person close to You, into Your loving arms and into Your arc of safety.

"In the mighty name of Jesus I pray. Amen."

The preacher seemed to be looking directly at Harold. "Today is the beginning of your new life. Right now, at this moment, God has shown His mercy on you and you have a new chance to begin again."

Harold would not have been able to explain it to anyone, but he did feel a touch from God, a comforting touch, a soothing touch. He looked at the gun on the dresser, a foreign object, and put it back in the strong box and locked it away. He didn't need to think about killing himself any more. He had a new beginning! God had a plan for his life! His life had just changed, at this very moment. He fell to his knees, cried out to God, and gave thanks.

## Patricia

"Mommy, wake up! Mommy, wake UP!"

"Wa-wa, wa-wa! Wa-wa, wa-WA!" Patricia was being pushed, shoved, moved around, and she didn't like it but she had no strength to fight it. An irritating voice was drilling into her head and she didn't want to take the effort to try to understand what those words meant. She just wanted to get some more sleep, but something – or someone – was pulling her out of it, back to this reality, this one that she did not particularly like; and here she was again. She felt as if she had been flattened to the floor for a long time. Her head was spinning and pounding as these interrupting sounds kept bombarding her from without and within.

She attempted to open her eyes, and the room was so bright, she had to scrunch them closed. She felt a movement. She was not alone in this place; another being had invaded her space.

"Mommy!" a shrill voice shouted. "Mommy, I'm hungry!"

She was a mommy. She acknowledged that. She had children. Her children were hungry. She was a bad mommy. She had not thought about her children in a long time. She had been gone on a long journey outside her own head, and who had been caring for them while she was gone? Where had they been? They were safe, weren't they? She really needed to think. How could she be a good mommy when she could not even think? Now that she was back here, she needed to think!

She forced her eyes to open, slowly, and examine her surroundings. The room was cold and empty, shredded linoleum in patches on the floor, a greasy black surface. Faded posters at odd angles were pinned to the walls in a failing effort to cover the many holes in the sheetrock. A doorway without a door led to another room where a door to the outside world stood wide open, lopsided on its hinges.

Patricia's eyes finally focused on her children, Kandy, Lesly and Lonny who were huddled in the corner of the room. She tried to smile at them, but her eyes filled with tears. They really shouldn't see her like this. Why were they here, in this God-forsaken place? Why was she in this place? Where exactly was she, anyway?

An urge from within her propelled her to the bathroom, a tiny, stinky place that hadn't been cleaned since the previous century, and she vomited violently into the toilet. She was surprised that her stomach had anything in it, but here it came, again and again.

"Mommy? Are you sick?" That was Kandy's voice, her oldest daughter, who was just four. Or had she turned five already? Kandy was the spokesperson of her children – Lonny and Lesly rarely spoke, except to each other.

"Yup. Mommy's sick," Patricia managed to say, in a growly voice that scratched her throat as she spoke. She pulled herself up to the sink so she could rinse out her mouth, but no water came from the faucet. Who could live in a place like this? It ought to be condemned. They needed to get home. She needed to take her children home.

But where was home? She could not picture their

home in her mind! Where did they live now? They had been moving from place to place, but where was their home now? Oh, no, oh no! She had been kicked out of that last little rat hole and since she didn't have any money, she had brought her children here, to a vacant house. It hadn't looked so bad in the dark. It hadn't seemed so bad when she was high. One of her buddies had fronted her some stuff, just a little, to get her by until she would get her next check, but her kids had not been here with her... or had they?

Well, she couldn't waste time trying to think about the past. She had to get her kids something to eat. She cringed at her next thought. She was going to have to go back to the one place she had said she would never go again – to her mother's.

## Jason

Jason Barney sat in the little office at the department store waiting for his interview. He was not really nervous, but he needed this job. Since his accident on his last job, he had not been able to work in construction. He had learned to let go of his anger, thanks to the counseling sessions with his pastor and the guidance of the Holy Spirit in his life. He knew the accident had not been his fault, but the cutting of corners in the area of safety; yet while he was recovering after his stay in the hospital, the slick lawyers who worked for his former boss had taken advantage of his weakened and confused state, leaving him liable not only for his own hospital bills, but also for the damage that had been caused on the job site.

In the very furthest corner of his mind, he had a tiny thought that the truth would be revealed and he would absolved of any wrongdoing, but in the meantime, he had to move on with his life. Now that he had most of his strength back, he could work hard, and he would, at even the most menial and insignificant job in the world. He had to get back into the swing of things, especially after being off work for so long. God had miraculously healed his broken back, and Jason was ready to move forward with whatever God had for him. He knew that he would never be able to pay his debts of more than one hundred thousand dollars while working at a job that paid minimum wage, but he had to start somewhere, and this was the place to start.

"Jason Barney?" a red-haired lady asked, popping her head through the door.

"Yes, I'm Jason," he said, smiling, standing and extending his hand.

"Follow me," she said, after a brief look of disgust at his hand.

He didn't let her discourage him. He knew that everyone had problems and her problems were not going to bother him. He followed her to a conference room where seven people were seated at a long table.

"Jason," an older man said, standing and reaching out his hand across the table. He also gave him a smile.

Jason shook his hand, relaxing a bit. "Yes, I am Jason Barney," he said, looking at each person at the table: four women and three men. The red-haired lady had left the room and he was glad about that. He didn't need her negative energy during his interview.

"Have a seat," the man said.

Jason sat in the only empty chair and smiled at the faces who were examining him. He thought about Jesus standing beside him and his confidence was fortified.

"We have looked at your resume and we are curious," the same man said. "Why do you want to work here?"

"Several reasons," Jason replied. "First of all, you are hiring. Secondly, I need a job, and third, I live just a few blocks from here, so I can walk to work. I have always liked this store, I shop here, and I feel that I can be a real asset to your company. I am a hard worker, I follow directions, and I work well as a team worker."

"It sounds like you just answered all our questions," another man said sarcastically.

Jason thought it was odd that they did not introduce themselves to him. He smiled at them.

"I think that is all we need to know," the first man said.

The group stood and began filing out of the room. Jason also stood.

"I just have one question," Jason said boldly. He couldn't let this opportunity pass. If he left now, they may never ask him to come back.

The first man who had spoken stopped and looked at him while the others, uninterested, left the two of them standing near the table.

"Yes?" the man asked, smiling at him pleasantly.

"When do you want me to start?" Jason asked.

"You can report to Alice in HR right now," the man said, gesturing with his head. "Down that hall, to the left. She will have your paperwork ready by the time you get there. You can start working this afternoon. Welcome aboard." He reached out to shake Jason's hand again, then he left.

Jason smiled to himself. That must have been the oddest job interview ever. He knew God was on his side, because things just didn't happen like that unless God was moving. Jason had the job! Before he left the room, he bowed his head in a prayer of thanksgiving. He couldn't wait to share his testimony with his church family!

## Chester

On Tuesday after dinner, Chester drove the eleven miles from his house to the church. His wife didn't usually come with him to Bible Studies, and he liked to be there every week – early. He wanted to be there before anyone else arrived, to unlock the doors, turn on the lights and the heat (unless it was warm enough for the air conditioner) and to just sit alone in the presence of God for awhile. His life did not offer him much time to himself. From the time he awakened at 5:30 a.m. on weekdays, Sandra was with him, fixing his breakfast and lunch, sitting with him at the table and cleaning up after him, until he left for work. His job site, the railroad station, was only a five-minute drive from his home, and there he was busy all day working alongside his co-workers, even eating his lunch with them. The minute he arrived back home, his wife had dinner ready for him and they would eat together while she relayed her drama of the day. After dinner, they sat side-by-side in their recliners in front of the TV where he would alternately read a magazine, watch whatever programs Sandra wanted to watch, and doze off. Saturdays were filled with chores, either at home or at the church, and on Sunday, he was with Sandra from the time they got out of bed until they got back in bed at night. Only on Tuesday evenings did he have some time to himself, usually thirty to forty minutes before Pastor arrived at the church. Chester never complained. God had given him a good life and he was very thankful. He could never ask for more.

He stepped into the sanctuary, feeling an instant sense of calmness, of sweetness enveloping him as he quietly pulled the door behind him. Suddenly he felt the sting of tears behind his eyes. He instinctively glanced around the room to be sure nobody saw them. Of course no one saw them – he was alone here, with the Lord. God had brought him and his wife to this church family years ago, in order to change their lives for the better.

He recalled the first time they had come to this church as visitors. His brother-in-law, Fuente, had invited them to come with him and his wife, Tammy, to church on a Sunday morning. Chester had been a little skeptical, aware that most churches just wanted to squeeze money out of the people who went there, but since Sandra had wanted to come with her sister, he had agreed. Their Sundays before church life had stretched out, long and boring, as they searched for a football game or movie on TV to fill their time, and they had spent long hours wasting the days away in their chairs.

When they first entered the church early that Sunday morning, before the service started, Chester had been surprised to see that the pastor was a black man and that the congregation was a mixture of black and white people. Fuente had not mentioned that fact, and Tammy probably hadn't even noticed. Chester had worked with a few black men but he had never really talked to them. Pastor Stronghart was different from those black men – as a matter of fact, the pastor was different from anyone Chester had ever met. He was open and friendly, inviting Chester and Sandra into the church as if they were guests in his home. Before the service even started, the pastor welcomed them and gave them a big hug, both together.

Chester had been overwhelmed by emotion, rolling

emotion he had not felt in a long time, maybe not ever in his life. He didn't need to look at Sandra to know that she was crying – really crying, tears falling from her eyes, not just that loud dramatic moaning she often did at home – and her cry was silent and unstoppable. The pastor himself took them to their seats in the pews where he introduced them to his wife and two children. Chester felt in his heart that they were now home, that this was the place they needed to be each and every Sunday. He wasn't sure what the church, the pastor and God had to offer them, but he knew they needed to keep coming here. He could feel a change in his life, in their lives, at that very moment. During their drive home after church, his wife agreed with him that Total Missionary Baptist Church was now their church home and she was also looking forward to returning the next Sunday.

Chester wasn't a great speaker or a master of words, but his pastor had found a niche for him and things for him to do around the church. He had acted as a handyman for the church, a janitor, a yard and garden specialist. He had brought people to church in his car and taken them back to their homes. He and his wife had become close to the pastor and his family. They took care of their children at various times when the pastor and his wife went out of town – the Lord had not blessed Chester and Sandra with children of their own – and a couple of years after they joined the church, they started coming to the pastor's house every Sunday for breakfast before church. The pastor's family was now their family, and Chester would do anything for them.

He walked through the sanctuary and went back to the kitchen, turning on the lights in each area on his way.

He glanced around to see if anything needed to be done, if anything needed to be cleaned or straightened. Anything he could do for the church building was something the pastor or his wife didn't have to do. He decided this would be a good time to clean out the refrigerator.

## Officer Shotgun

On his way to the precinct, Officer Shotgun decided to drive by that church again. He had been so busy this month with seven robberies, nineteen burglaries, and seventeen accidents on his beat, he had not had a chance to go by there since that Sunday a few weeks ago. He knew something illegal had to be going on in there, and he was going to find out just what it was.

As he slowed down in front of the building, it looked like all the lights were on inside, although there was only one car in the parking lot. Nobody was shouting or singing now. He noticed the sign near the door with the service times. This evening they had something scheduled called "Bible Studies." That was a laugh. Who, in this day and age, would ever study an archaic book like the Bible? Everyone knew that old book was outdated and untrue. This must be a cover for some kind of drug distribution setting, or maybe it was a set up for a financial scam. Whatever was happening here, he had to know. He didn't think he could catch anyone in the act today, but he would be back, and no matter how long it took, he would do whatever he needed to do to get this fraudulent operation out of this neighborhood forever. Right now he had to go pick up his partner so they could make their rounds. He mentally placed this church on the top of his list of suspicious places as he drove around the corner.

## Carolina

Today her apartment was somewhat organized and Carolina was proud of herself. She had gotten newspapers, magazines, letters, books, mail, catalogs and recipes into piles on her floor and coffee table. She now had clear paths to the kitchen, bathroom, bedroom, sewing room, and front door. She had worked hard, concentrating and staying focused on her task, which had taken all day to complete. She looked over her work with satisfaction – until, wait! What was that newspaper on the floor, out of place? She reached with her cane, stretched her arm, leaned toward it, and was finally able to scoot the paper to a spot where she could reach down and grab it. What in the world – how could this be? The newspaper article about that church, the one with the big color photo, was back out of the trash again! How many times did she have to throw it away?

Carolina was a sensible woman, a logical woman, and she knew two things for sure: the newspaper didn't get out of her garbage can by itself; and there could be no profit for her to even think about going to church. Those two statements didn't seem to make sense at this point, because maybe, just maybe, God who was trying to get her attention, and that was not logical. It did not fit with anything she knew.

She looked at the photo again, the crumpled page with the people praying inside a church. Did they really think someone was listening to their prayers? Why did they all have a look of inner peace on their faces, in their postures? Did they know something she didn't know? She could do some investigating. She needed a project. She didn't have anything else going on until the sixth of the month when she would get her food coupons and could go to the store, and this would be something to motivate her to get out of the house and meet some new people. Her car was sitting in the parking lot, and she could drive to the church tomorrow, Wednesday, when they had a noon prayer service. As a matter of fact, she decided to write it on her calendar, a firm appointment that she would keep. She needed to discover what unseen force was directing her to this church!

## William

The temperature had dropped and William Dorsett shivered. He was cold inside his own house. He hadn't been able to pay the gas bill, and he couldn't use the oven to warm the house – he had to stretch the electricity as long as he could. He wasn't good with finances. His mom had always taken care of everything. Even during the past years when she was bedridden with diabetes and he was paid to be her caregiver, she had taken care of the bills. She had made sure everything was paid on time. He had been such a fool to spend money on a new TV, money that she had told him to use to pay her life insurance policy. How could he have known she was going to die? Now he no longer got her check or his check, and he was nearly sixty years old, too old to train for a new job. He didn't have any income. What was he going to do? How was he going to survive? Would he really lose his mom's house? He had no idea what to do.

His phone rang, startling him. He wasn't expecting that it would still work – wasn't that another overdue bill? He pushed himself off the sofa to go answer it.

"Hello?" he said tentatively, ready to hang up if the caller were a creditor.

"Brother William!" a voice said cheerfully.

"Pastor Stronghart?" William asked, relieved.

"Yes! I was just thinking about you and God put it on my heart to give you a call. How are you doing?"

William didn't know how to answer. He was not doing well, but he was afraid to admit it. He didn't want

Pastor Stronghart to think he was a failure. He and his mom had been members of that church for twenty years, although they had not been able to attend for quite some time. Pastor Stronghart and his wife and other church members had visited his mom regularly, to encourage her, to have Bible studies with her and to give her communion. How could he tell his pastor that everything was falling apart, that he was about to lose his mom's house? Yet he could not lie to his pastor – that would be a real sin. He had to get up his courage to tell him the truth.

"To be honest with you, Pastor, I'm not doing very well," he said slowly.

"Are you sick?"

"No, I'm not sick."

"Do you want to talk about it?" His pastor sounded genuinely concerned.

"I do, but…" he didn't feel like talking about it right now. He had to figure some things out, but his mind was all jumbled with everything he had to do, and trying to think of everything he had not been doing.

"How about if I come and get you a little later and take you for a cup of coffee?"

"Yes. Yes, that would be great," William said. "I would like that." Coffee was warm and that sounded good. He knew that they would be able to talk, and he would have a chance to think about it and figure out what he was going to tell his pastor. "Today?"

"Yes, I'll come over this afternoon, if that fits in with your schedule."

"Thank you so much, Pastor. I look forward to seeing you."

"See you later, then. God bless you, Brother William."

His circumstances had not changed, but his attitude had. He knew his pastor would have a solution to his problem, or, at least, some good advice for him.

## Evelyn

Evelyn Sooner walked aimlessly around her house. She didn't have anything to do. The house was spotless, so clean that a visitor might think no one even lived here. Evelyn sort of felt that way, now that she was living alone here. She just couldn't get used to the emptiness she felt, now that her daughter, Marilyn, had gone off to college. They had spent so many hours together, evening after evening, talking about everything under the sun. They had a great relationship, but now she was gone.

Evelyn tried to look on the bright side. Marilyn wasn't dead – she was just away at college. She was with her friends, studying and learning and preparing herself for her fantastic future. She was happy and healthy… and Evelyn was alone.

She thought back to the nightly walks they had taken during the summer before Marilyn had left. The summer had been hot and muggy, so just as the sun was setting, they would leave the house for a long walk, several miles, at least, and talk. Marilyn would ask questions. Evelyn would tell about her mother, her grandmother, her childhood, her experiences in college. The conversations were so in-depth and so fulfilling, Evelyn did not really consider that they were going to end. She had been excited to drive Marilyn and her suitcases and her laptop to college, and even on the two-hour drive home, she was still so happy for her daughter. It was actually about a month later when reality shocked her: Marilyn wasn't coming home. Oh, sure, she would visit for a weekend every once in a while, but she was not going to be living with her mother ever again. Evelyn now lived alone. Evelyn was going to be living alone, in this house, forever.

She avoided her daughter's room and walked out onto the patio. She would not have an opportunity to work overtime. She didn't have the energy to get another job to fill in the empty time slots in her life. She wasn't motivated enough to take a class at the community college. She didn't feel like cooking or eating and she had no energy to exercise or take fitness classes at the Y. She tried to do a little reading but she had a hard time concentrating – especially since she was so emotional. She either felt like she was on the verge of crying or she felt nothing at all, just blah.

Was she walking in circles or just pacing the floor? Did anything really matter? Nothing was as important as it had been before. She no longer needed to cook meals or decorate the house for her daughter, and she did not need those things for herself. Food no longer had any taste for her. Nothing was interesting to her anymore. She did not need time to 'do her own thing.' She needed a person in her life.

She needed a hobby. What kind of hobby could she start that didn't cost anything? All of her finances were going toward Marilyn's education, to avoid the dreaded student loan that could cause financial problems for the remainder of both of their lives. She had to find something to do, some kind of distraction, yet something that would be fulfilling. The ideal hobby would be something she could do on her own, alone, and not rely on anyone. Another person, no matter who it was, no matter what commitment he or she made, could desert her at any time, leaving Evelyn alone once again. No, she had to find something else, something important.

Maybe she should ask her pastor for advice. He was really busy, but he was also concerned for each of his church members. Although she had not been going to church for awhile, hers was a pastor who knew every member of his congregation, and he remembered everything about them. Maybe he knew where she could volunteer, just a little, to give her something to do. Yes, she would call him tomorrow; or better yet, she could stop by the church and talk to him.

She began to feel a little bit better, just knowing she had a plan, a good plan. A fat tear for her daughter fell from her left eye, but that one tear was mixed in with a bit of optimism.

## Patricia

Patricia kept postponing the inevitable. She knew she had to take her kids to her mom's house, but knowing and doing were two different things. They were hungry and she was broke. The vacant house was just barely a roof over their heads and they needed so much more than that. She had to wait at least three weeks before she would get her welfare money, and her food coupons had been traded away as soon as she had gotten them, since she had borrowed against them. After being sober for nearly two days, she could see how thin her kids were getting, and how thin their clothing was. They were so quiet, staring at her with big, buggy eyes, waiting quietly for her to take care of them – and she couldn't!

She could not get a job. She had no skills. She had not completed high school, and she couldn't go to work anywhere and leave three preschoolers alone. The little bit of money the state gave her didn't go very far, and this month it had disappeared in just one night of her own private celebration, her rebellion against the system when she gave in to her temptation and met up with her dealer. She had bought her kids McDonald's and herself a good fix. She had not been able to plan beyond that one night, thinking that things would somehow work themselves out.

Her mother's voice popped into her head: "Failing to plan is planning to fail."

"Shut up!" Patricia shouted. She did not want to hear her mother criticizing her, and that is exactly what she would have to hear, beginning the second she stepped into her mother's home.

"Okay, Mommy," Kandy said quietly, cowering together with her brother and her sister in the corner of the cold, filthy room.

"No, I didn't mean you," Patricia sobbed. She could not hold herself together any longer, not even in front of her children. As they stared at her, she began to cry. They looked at her in shock. She had to muster up the courage to take them from this awful place, to get them to a place where somebody could take care of them, somebody who loved them. Didn't she love them enough? Yes, but love alone was not enough for them. They needed food. They needed warm clothing.

Suddenly she felt like laughing. Why was it, any time she had money and wanted to get high, someone would instantly show up to take her to where she wanted to go? She didn't even have to ask for a ride, one would simply be there for her. Now that she needed to take her kids to their grandma's home, no one was around. She had no idea how to contact anyone who could do her a favor. They would have to walk nearly four miles across town to get to her mother's apartment.

They had to do it, right now. She could carry Lesly part of the way, but none of them had much strength, since they had not eaten anything in a couple of days. Instantly she was energized, needing to get away from here immediately. The last thing she needed was to be arrested for trespassing in a vacant, run-down house that probably had been condemned. Then her kids would surely be taken away from her. She could not let that happen!

"Come on, let's go," she said, making a lifting motion with her hands towards Kandy, Lonny and Lesly. They stared at her, frozen, unsure of what their mother was telling them, afraid of what this sudden change of mood was all about. "Come on! We are getting out of here right now!"

She opened the door, wobbly on its hinges, and looked outside. The weather wasn't lovely. Rain was sure to fall soon. However, they had to get going at this very moment, to get out of this house before some terrible fate came upon them.

"Mommy, I'm hungry," Kandy said, getting to her feet. She helped her little brother and sister, and they walked holding hands to the doorway, where their mother was standing and staring.

"Yes, we all are," Patricia said absentmindedly. She knew where her mother's apartment was, but she had not been there since Kandy was a baby. Patricia could not picture in her mind the route to her mother's place. Her sense of direction was all mixed up and she wasn't sure of her current location. Nothing in this neighborhood looked familiar. What was that red building across the street, anyway? How had they gotten here? More importantly, how could they get away from here?

She did not know her mother's telephone number. She didn't have a phone to call her, anyway. What was she going to do? Nothing ever worked out right for her! Why was life a constant struggle, a moment-by-moment fight against the elements that were always beating her down? Which way should they go?

"Where we going, Mommy?" Kandy asked.

"Yeah, yeah, just be quiet and let Mommy think," Patricia said. Her daughter's voice was such a source of irritation, that shrill sound grating on the brain. "We are going for a walk," she finally answered. "Come on, before it starts raining."

She scooped Lesly into her arms and walked across the muddy yard to the street. She stopped and looked to the sky, as if the route might be drawn in the clouds. Kandy and Lonny bumped into their mother's legs.

"God, a little guidance would work pretty good for me right about now," she said to the sky. She closed her eyes for a few seconds, trying to feel which way would lead them in the right direction. All she needed to do was to see something familiar so she could know the way to go. When she opened her eyes, she didn't have a clear answer, so she decided to go with her gut feeling. They would just start walking down this street and eventually she would know where they were, and then she could get them to her mother's place.

## Pastor Stronghart

The clouds were dumping rain in the neighborhood of the church, but that did not deter Pastor Stronghart from going to Noon Prayer. He never cancelled a service. He wanted to be sure the doors were open, in case somebody needed to come in for prayer – and almost every week, somebody did. Even if no one else showed up, he wanted the church doors to be open, just in case God led that one person in need to the church.

He parked his car in the long driveway on the side of the church and splashed through the deep water to get to the back door. The key stuck in the lock, so he jiggled and lifted and pushed and pulled until the key turned and he opened the door.

The inside of the building was damp and clammy. He turned up the thermostat and kept his coat on, knowing this old building would not be instantly warm. He turned on the lights in the sanctuary, unlocked the front door and looked outside. The rain was still pouring, flowing down the street like two little rivers, one on each side of the road. He propped the door open and sat on the front pew with his Bible in his lap. Before he began to read, he let the song in his heart come up out of his mouth, and he started singing praises to God.

"My God is real, for I can feel Him in my soul," he sang. He set the Bible on the seat and he stood up, lifting his hands and singing wholeheartedly. He kept singing, and when he finished that song, he started another. He was all wrapped up in praising God, thanking Him and magnifying His name, lifted to another plane, to higher heights, so when he opened his eyes and turned around, he was surprised to see a woman sitting in the back pew. He hadn't heard her come in, but now the door was closed, so she must have closed it behind her.

"Good afternoon!" he said enthusiastically, walking toward her. He had never seen this woman before. She was very large and she was very wet. He extended his hand to her. "I'm Pastor Stronghart," he said. "Welcome to Total Missionary Baptist Church."

"My name is Carolina," she said gruffly. She barely touched his hand in a return shake.

"Welcome, Sister Carolina," he said with a big smile. "You are just in time for our Wednesday Noon Prayer time."

"That is why I came here in the first place," she said. She did not return his smile.

"Then you are definitely in the right place," he said.

"I saw your picture in the newspaper," she barked.

"Oh, you saw the article about the church?" he asked, trying to soften her rough exterior. He could see another emotion beneath the bitterness she displayed.

"I saw it and I threw it in the trash," she said, a tiny smile beginning to form. "Then somehow it came back out, so I threw it away again. It kept coming back, no matter how many times I threw it away, and I couldn't get rid of it!"

Pastor Stronghart smiled but he didn't interrupt her. He sensed that she had a lot more to say.

"I eventually decided that it must have a message for

me, so I had to come here and find out what was going on here, and why I should come here." She let out a sigh, as if she hadn't spoken to anyone in a long time. "So now, here I am. I guess I am supposed to be here, but I still don't know why."

"You just got here," Pastor Stronghart said. "I think you will know why you are here after a while."

She looked at him suspiciously. "Why do YOU think I am here?"

"Because this is where God wants you to be," he said certainly. He had no doubt.

## Carolina

Carolina's mouth dropped open. This was something she had never considered. She had always thought of God as some Being who was up in outer space or heaven or somewhere, but not as Someone who cared where she was or what she did. She had never known Him to be present in her life, as He had let horrible things happen to her. She had always had to handle every situation herself, without any help from anyone. She wanted to argue with this pastor – she was really good at winning arguments, since she would not let up until the other person gave in – but somehow she *felt* he was telling the truth. She had never felt anything like what she was feeling at this moment. She should be scared, but instead, she felt strangely comforted.

"H-h-how do you know?" she finally stammered, her arguing words having slipped away from her.

"You would not be here if God didn't want you here," he answered. "God has something special for you here."

She kind of panicked, thinking this man was going to try to convince her to give him all of her money, because, what else could be his motivation? He was a pastor, yes, but did he really want to help her?

"Like what?" she asked, trying to regain control of the conversation.

"Like healing, for one," he said softly. He sat in the pew across from her. "God can heal those hurts that you have been holding deep inside of you. He wants to heal you."

She didn't want to let herself cry here, not now. She had not cried in front of anyone since she was a little girl and her father had taught her that crying was a sign of weakness, and he had beat her until she was able to control her tears. The few times she had cried since then, she had been sure to be alone, where no one could see nor hear her.

She tried to say something, but her words got choked in her throat. This man just sat, patiently waiting. She thought about the fact that she had not been alone in a room with a man in at least thirty years, and now she was not afraid. She felt almost comfortable with him. She shook her head, unable to speak.

"Have you ever accepted Jesus as your personal Savior?" he asked, looking directly into her eyes. His eyes looked very kind and understanding.

"I don't know," she whispered, looking at the floor. She didn't know what he meant by that.

"What do you know about Jesus?" he asked.

She had no idea what this had to do with anything, but she answered quietly, "I remember reading that He was the Son of God and He died on the cross for our sins."

"The Bible says, in Romans 10:9, 'that if you confess with your mouth the Lord Jesus and believe in your heart that God has raised Him from the dead, you will be saved.' Do you believe that on the third day, after He was crucified, that He was raised from the dead?"

"Yes, on Easter, He rose from the dead," she said.

"Then you are saved! Jesus is your personal Savior," Pastor Stronghart said. "Jesus said, in John 14:14, and

He is talking to Christians, to saved people, 'If you ask anything in My name, I will do it.' Sister Carolina, you can ask God for anything, according to His will, and He will do it for you."

She had never heard that before. She didn't know much about the Bible, except the few Bible stories she had learned as a child: Jonah and the whale, David and Goliath, and Jesus feeding five thousand people with a little boy's lunch; and that one seemed pretty far-fetched to her. Maybe some day she could ask Pastor Stronghart about it, but now was not the time. She surely had never thought God would do something in her life, or that He even cared about her.

"Oh," was all she could think of to say, her mind suddenly opened to possibilities she had never considered before.

"God can heal you, right now," Pastor Stronghart said.

She nodded, looking down at her lap. She didn't want him to see her cry, because that was about to happen.

"It's prayer time," the pastor said quietly.

From what she knew about prayer, this would be a time they would sit with their heads bowed and pray a silent prayer. She nodded her head and closed her eyes, pulling her purse close to her, since she would not be able to keep an eye on it while her eyes were closed. A loud voice interrupted her thoughts – she didn't know how to even start to say a prayer.

"Father, in the name of Jesus, we come to You this afternoon," the pastor said loudly.

Carolina opened one eye, just peeking, because he

sounded to be so far away from her. He was standing in front of the pews, not up in the pulpit, but on the main floor.

"We just want to say, 'thank You,' because You have been so good to us," he continued. "You have given us another day to thank You, another day to praise You, another day to come to You with all of our problems. We come lifting up Your holy name. Oh, heavenly Father, we pray now for Sister Carolina, who came into the house of the Lord today, not by accident, not by coincidence, because we know You have everything perfectly planned. Father, You knew from the day she was born that she would be coming here today, and we know You have all power, healing power, loving power, the power to make her whole once again, in You. We know You have a plan for her life, a plan to use her for Your purpose, starting right now, today, as she feels a healing touch from You.

"Father, we pray, Lord God, for the ones that had a desire to be here and are not today. Oh, heavenly Father, we thank You, right now. Touch, Lord God, every part of our services, every meeting that takes place in this building. We pray, Lord God, that You will get the glory, in Jesus name; not my will, but Thy will be done. Now Lord, bless us in a mighty way. In the name of Jesus we pray, and we give you glory right now, in Jesus' name. Thank God, thank God, thank God."

Carolina opened her eyes and didn't see the pastor anywhere. She looked around the room. Where had he gone? Did he somehow slip out while he was praying? Then he startled her when she saw him getting up off his knees.

"How are you feeling now, Sister?" he asked.

She was feeling better, and she felt surprisingly like family to this man when he called her 'Sister.'

"Can I talk to you for a few minutes?" she asked. She now didn't feel so bold, like she could merely speak her mind to make her point, but she felt loved and respected.

"Of course, Sister Carolina," he said kindly, coming to sit near her on the next pew.

"This has to be in confidence," she said, biting her lower lip. "I have never told anyone this." She wasn't sure why she wanted to tell him, but she just needed to. "My father," she began, deciding that she could let a tear fall, that she didn't need to hold it in any longer, "he abused me when I was a child. He hurt me and I hated him. I ran away from home and I never went back until after he died, more than twenty years ago. I really did love him, and I never told him that because I was too afraid of him. He hurt me so badly. I am so sorry, but I can't tell him." She became aware that she was crying, in front of this stranger, this pastor, and she was not ashamed.

"And you have been holding in those feelings all these years," the pastor said gently. "Now you can let them go. Your heavenly Father has forgiven you. You can forgive your earthly father. You can be healed of this hurt."

"There are so many things I never got to tell him," she said. "He didn't know I went to nursing school and became a nurse. He didn't know that another man – a doctor – raped me and I had a daughter. She is all grown up now and she has a daughter, but I haven't seen her in years. I tried so hard to be a good parent, but I had a hard time doing it all by myself."

"You were not doing it all by yourself," the pastor said. "God was always there with you."

"But He didn't help me!" she protested.

"Did you ask for His help?"

She hung her head. "No, I didn't. I didn't even know He was there."

"Well, you know He is with you now, don't you?" he asked gently.

She nodded. "What should I do now?"

"What do you think you should do?"

"I could write him a letter," she said, "to my father, not to God, I mean."

"I think that is a great idea," the pastor said encouragingly.

"I could tell him everything I never told him before," she said. She really needed to get it all out, to let it all go, so she could focus on her current life, as the pastor had said. "But then, what can I do with the letter? I can't mail it to heaven," she said, thinking, if her father *was* in heaven. He might have gone to that other place, but she couldn't mail it there either.

"Write the letter," the pastor said, as he stood and walked toward the front of the church, "seal it in an envelope, and you can put it in here, in our prayer box." He lifted up a small box that was covered with blue fabric, with gold lettering that read 'Our Blessing Box.'

"That is what I will do," she said resolutely, so thankful to have ahead of her a closing door to her past. She had never told anyone, not even her mother, what her father had done to her, but now, with God's help, she would finally be able to let it all go.

The front door to the church opened and a cold, damp wind blew a lady inside the sanctuary.

"Good afternoon, Sister Evelyn!" the pastor said enthusiastically, genuinely happy to see her. Maybe some day he would be that happy to see Carolina, too.

## Evelyn

"Hi, Pastor Stronghart," she said, as she shook the cold and the water off her.

The pastor gave Evelyn a big hug, then stepped back to introduce the lady who was sitting in the back pew.

"Sister Evelyn, this is Sister Carolina," he said.

"Hello," Evelyn said, reaching out to shake hands with this large lady. "Nice to meet you."

"Nice to meet you, too," Carolina said, her voice fading at the last couple of words.

"We have already started our prayer time," Pastor Stronghart said, "but it is never too late for prayer."

"Pastor, I have a problem," Evelyn blurted out, not intending to just say it like that. After all, her problem was so minor compared with problems other people had, but this one was consuming her.

"Nothing is too hard for God," he reminded her.

Evelyn glanced briefly at Carolina, who obviously wasn't going anywhere. Well, it didn't matter who knew about this problem; Evelyn just needed an answer, help from her pastor.

"You know my daughter, Marilyn, left to go to college a few weeks ago, right?" she began.

"Yes, yes, of course!" Pastor Stronghart said. "Is she in trouble? Does she need anything?"

"No, nothing like that," Evelyn answered. "She is doing fine. She's doing great." Suddenly her problem seemed to be so selfish. Shouldn't she be so thankful that her daughter was doing well? She was thankful – but she was also lonely. "It's just that, well, ever since she left, well, she was like my best friend, and we talked about everything. Now, it's only been a few weeks, but we never talk anymore; I mean, only for a few minutes, and then she has to go because she's so busy…" She had not planned to cry! Something about being in the church building made her emotions come to the surface, and she finally let the tears fall, to match the rain that she could hear pounding on the roof.

"You miss her," Pastor Stronghart said, "and that is understandable. You raised her alone, and you two have been together, raising each other. I remember when she was just a small child and you brought her to be dedicated to the Lord, right here. Has she found a church home near the college yet?"

"No, I don't think so," Evelyn answered, holding back a sob. "I think she is so involved with her new classes and schedule that she hasn't had time to think about church."

"She was raised in the church, and she will be fine," Pastor Stronghart assured her. "Proverbs 22:6 tells us, 'train up a child in the way he should go: and when he is old, he will not depart from it.' So you don't need to worry about her. She is going to be all right."

"But what about me?" Evelyn cried. "I need something to do, something to think about, something to occupy my mind."

"How often have you been reading your Bible?" Pastor Stronghart asked.

Evelyn felt guilty. She could not remember the last

time she opened her Bible. She wasn't even sure where it was. She had brought it last time she came to church, which was a few months before Marilyn had left.

"Not often," she confessed, slowly sitting on a pew.

"How often?" Pastor Stronghart pressed. "Once a week? Once a month?"

"Not often," she repeated, looking down at her hands.

"I can think of several ministries where you could get involved," he said, "but the first and most important thing is for you to get grounded in the Word of God." He walked up to the podium and picked up some papers. "Both of you ladies should start on this Bible studies course," he said, handing a packet to each of them. "This has a daily Bible-reading schedule and notes and outlines for each book as you study. This is just the first month of study. Come out on Tuesday nights to our Bible Studies class and we can go over any questions you have, either in the study or about the Bible in general. I recommend that you stick with the reading schedule. Don't try to get ahead, just stay on the daily schedule and meditate on what you read every day. And do the scheduled reading every day, so you won't fall behind. Most importantly, make sure you pray each time before you start to study, to ask the Holy Spirit to open up the spiritual truths of His Word."

Evelyn had not thought about praying before reading her Bible, but it made sense to ask God for His guidance while reading His word.

"Studying the Word of God is feeding yourself spiritually," Pastor Stronghart continued. "If you go without eating physical food for one day, you begin to feel physically weak, right?"

Both ladies nodded.

"If you go one day without reading and studying the Word of God, you begin to be spiritually weak. This Bible studies course will give you a good start to spiritual strength, and, Sister Evelyn, I have no doubt that the Lord will soon direct you to the ministry that is perfect for you, and will glorify Him. Because that should be our ultimate goal, to glorify Him. Don't you agree?"

"Yes, Pastor," Evelyn said, feeling enlightened. She had been so closed off, so entangled in her own problems, she had not even thought that the answer could be as close as studying the Bible. She had enjoyed Bible studies when she and Marilyn had been coming to the Tuesday evening classes while Marilyn was a young teenager. Then they had gotten so busy, that was one of the tasks that had dropped off her list. Now it was time to pick it up again, she was sure of it.

The door of the church burst open and a young man plunged into the room.

"Hey, Pastor Stronghart!" he shouted. "Sorry I am late to prayer meeting!"

## Jason

"Good afternoon, Brother Jason," Pastor Stronghart said, coming to give him a hug.

"I'm a little wet," Jason apologized.

"A little wet?" Pastor Stronghart asked, hugging him anyway. "I would say that you are drenched!"

"It is raining," Jason said, stating the obvious.

"Brother Jason, I want you to meet Sister Evelyn and Sister Carolina," Pastor Stronghart said, making Jason aware that there were others in the sanctuary. One lady was sitting in the back pew to his right, another lady was in the pew in front of her.

"Nice to meet you," he said loudly, drying his right hand, before shaking hands with each of them.

"Nice meeting you," one of the ladies said. The larger lady just nodded to him.

"Pastor Stronghart, I have a testimony," he said, so excited he felt about to burst. He stepped into the pew to his left but didn't sit down.

"Go ahead and testify, Brother Jason," Pastor Stronghart said.

"You know I had a job interview," he said, then turned to the ladies. "Oh, you two don't know, but I had a job interview yesterday. I used to work in construction, but then I was involved in an accident on the job, and off from work for more than a year, in and out of the hospital and stuff, recovering, and I thought I might not ever get a job again. For reasons I do not want to mention right now,

I can't work in construction any more, but one of my friends turned me on to this church. He brought me here, and I was blown away! I accepted Jesus as my Savior and I was baptized a year ago, and God has really been working in my life, really, ever since the first day I came here. I have seen miracles, in my life, in my family, wow, but I have to tell you what happened yesterday at the job interview!" He looked at his pastor, his smile spreading across his face.

"Praise God! What happened to me would be unbelievable to a person who is not aware of what God can do," he continued. He could feel his smile spreading across his entire face.

"But we know what God can do!" Pastor Stronghart added, "and that is anything but fail. Go ahead, Brother Jason. Tell us how God moved in the interview."

"Well, that's just it," Jason continued, still baffled by what had happened. "I get into the room with, like, seven other people, all of them sitting there, looking at me so seriously, and I sit down, and I am thinking, Jesus, You are right here with me, and they ask me why I want to work there. I just tell them, 'you are hiring, I need a job, and I live close to here,' and then I'm waiting for the questions to start. But instead, the guy tells me I have the job! The hard part is already over, and I started working yesterday afternoon! Praise God, they hired me just like that!" He snapped his fingers.

"God is in the miracle-working business," Pastor Stronghart confirmed, waving his hand in the air.

"I was praising God all afternoon," Jason said, "and the other thing is, my boss came while I was working and told me I can have off Sundays to go to church! I didn't even ask for that."

"Really?" Evelyn asked, her eyes widening.

"Before we ask, God answers," Pastor Stronghart said. "That's in the Word. You ladies will soon discover that, along with a lot of other great things, as you work through the Bible study lessons. Brother Jason, I just gave them each a copy of the first installment of our Bible studies course."

"Oh, you are going to love it!" Jason said, looking at the two ladies, who were both a lot older than he was. He could see an emptiness, a hunger, in their eyes, and he knew they both needed the Word of God to move in their lives.

"I have been studying every day since I started coming here, for the past year, and I tell you, it is fantastic. Studying the Bible will change your life, I am not kidding you. A whole new part of you will open up that you never even knew about. Your spiritual life will come alive. God did it for me, and I know He will do it for you, if you apply yourself and really study. And it doesn't really take up that much time to study. Just make it a practice to set aside some time every day, thirty minutes to an hour, to study His Word, and you will be amazed at what God will accomplish in your life. He will use you in ways you never dreamed of. He will put you in situations where you know it is the Lord, and you will be there to help other people, or maybe just to give someone an encouraging word. I could tell you about so many times and ways God has used me, only because I am open to what He wants me to do."

"Brother Jason, you are a walking testimony," Pastor Stronghart said.

"Pastor, I have to tell it like it is," he said, shrugging his shoulders.

"Sisters, this young man is only twenty-five years old, and he is truly on fire for the Lord. So many people wait until they are older to come to the Lord, and by then, many of them are too weak or too tired or too beat down to do any kind of service for the Lord. Brother Jason has yielded himself to the Lord and to the leading of His Holy Spirit, and God has been using him to do great things every day."

"Yeah, and the best thing, I even led my mom to the saving knowledge of Jesus Christ," Jason said, so thankful in his heart that God had opened that door for him. "She comes here sometimes for Sunday morning worship. You will probably meet her, if you come to Sunday services." He stopped there, not wanting to offend these two ladies. He was hoping to be inviting, to share the goodness of God, but he didn't want to scare them away from the church or make them feel like he thought they had to be there on Sundays, even though he did. He wanted the Spirit of God to bring them on Sundays. If any other person brought them to church, they would only come when that person was coming. If they were led to church by the Spirit of God, they would continue to come, because they would know God wanted them to be there.

## Carolina

Carolina didn't know what to make of this young man. She was drawn to him, to his fire, to his energy, to his enthusiasm. This was the type of person she would love to have in her life. She wondered if the other members of this congregation were as excited about life as he was. He was so positive about his situation, so positive about everything, even though he said he had spent a lot of time in the hospital. He had undoubtedly made a complete recovery, and he seemed to be making the most of his life.

She looked at the papers the pastor had given her. She had a Bible at home, somewhere, and maybe working on answering these questions would help fill her endless days alone in her apartment. She tuned out the conversation between Evelyn, Jason and the pastor as she stuffed the pages into her oversized purse. She was already beginning to form the letter to her father in her mind, and she wanted to get home and get started on writing it. She had plenty of time to work on these two tasks. They would keep her busy. And if studying the Bible did make a change in her life, well, it could only change for the better. She was looking forward to something new and good in her life.

"I have to get going now," she said, struggling to her feet, interrupting their discussion. "I have to get home." She had no other explanation – she just had to go, and she had to go right now.

Pastor Stronghart was by her side in an instant, giving her a brotherly hug. "I am so glad that the Spirit of God brought you here today, Sister Carolina," he said. "You are welcome to come back any time the doors are open.

Do you sing? We have choir rehearsal tomorrow evening, and we would love to have you join us."

She burst out laughing. "No, I can't sing," she said. "You would not want me to break all of your eardrums."

"Do you play the piano?" he asked. She could tell he was being sincere, but she was not in any way musically inclined.

"No, I don't, but my daughter..." she stopped. Patty had played piano when she was younger, or at least she had taken lessons for three years, but Carolina had no idea where Patty was. "No, I can't play the piano," she clarified.

"Well, you are welcome to come here any time," he repeated. "Can I help you to your car?"

"Pastor, I can help her," Jason said, stepping over to open the door. "Wow, it is still raining really hard," he remarked. "Pastor, do you have an umbrella?"

"I have one in my bag," Carolina said. She leaned against the pew as she dug out her portable umbrella.

"Here, let me hold it over you," Jason said, surprising Carolina with his charitable nature. Most young people these days just pushed her out of the way or taunted her because she was so slow-moving.

"Thank you, Jason," she said, stepping through the open door. He held the umbrella over her head, not over himself, and she was not getting at all wet, even in this pouring rain.

"No problem, Sister Carolina," he replied, as if he were talking to his own sister. "God put me here to serve."

She made it all the way to the car without getting wet and she handed her car key to Jason. "Can you unlock it for me?"

"Sure thing," he said, unlocking the door and opening it for her. "I really hope you come back to TMBC," he said, still holding the umbrella over her, until she was able to get into the driver's seat.

"TMBC?" she asked, puzzled.

"Total Missionary Baptist Church," he explained. "Yeah, God can really use you here, to do great things for Him."

"I can't really do anything," she began to protest.

"Maybe not, but God can use you and He can do things through you, using your hands, your feet, your brain, to glorify Him and to bring others to Him."

Carolina was skeptical about this, but since Jason was being so nice to her, she decided to not argue with him. "Well, I will probably see you again sometime," she finally said.

"I hope to see you on Sunday," he said, making her feel like he really did want her to come to Sunday service. He closed her umbrella and handed it to her.

"Okay, Sunday. I will see you Sunday morning," she promised.

As she started her car and began driving home, she found herself to be excited about something for the first time in years. She had an appointment on Sunday, and someone wanted her to be there!

## Patricia

"Mommy, I'm cold," Kandy cried, tugging on her mother's soaked sweatshirt.

"Hungry," Lonny added.

Patricia dared not look at them as she hoisted Lesly higher on her hip. They just reminded her that she was a bad mom, dragging them out in the stormy weather like this. It had not been storming when they left that condemned house, but now they were so far away from it, they would have to keep on going until they arrived at her mother's apartment.

She also was cold, hungry and tired, and they had been walking for hours in the rain. It was just her luck, her bad luck, to be walking all this time and not see anyone she knew to give her a ride. She was pretty sure she was going in the direction of her mother's house, but at the moment they were in an awful neighborhood. She knew this neighborhood well – it was the best place to easily find anything she needed, when she had money. When she did not have any money, no one in this area wanted anything to do with her, and she made it a practice to stay as far from here as possible. This was not an area to bring children; yet, here she was, with them, in this terrible area, in the pouring rain.

"Mommy, can we stop now? I'm tired," Kandy complained.

"Do you see any place where we can stop?" Patricia shouted at her daughter, immediately sorry for her reaction, as the water ran down her back. Her hair was soaked, her face was soaked, her clothes were soaked. She could not let them stop walking, even for a minute, because she knew she would start shivering and probably never be able to stop.

"Can we go to that lighthouse?" Kandy asked. "It looks warm over there."

"Lighthouse?" Patricia asked. "There are no lighthouses in this whole town," she said, confused, as she trudged along the cracked and broken sidewalk.

"Right over there!" Kandy said, letting go of her mother's clothing.

Patricia heard the splash of a little foot in a big puddle and turned around to see Kandy starting to walk across the street that had running rivers of water down each side.

"Kandy!" she shouted, as a car came zooming down the street, splashing and drenching them with muddy water. The driver did not slow the car at all, apparently not even seeing the little girl in the street.

Patricia tried to leap over the huge puddle but missed, landing in the deep water, with Lonny following close behind her as they all crossed the street to the other side. They were soaked to the skin – they could not be any more wet than they were. She looked at the building ahead of them, so out of place in this neighborhood – a small church that was so brightly lit, she knew why Kandy had called it a lighthouse.

Kandy was boldly walking up the steps to the front door. Patricia followed her daughter. Even if they could just stay on the front porch, out of the rain and away from the wind, that would be better than being out in the midst of the elements. She pulled Lonny's hand as they mounted the steps, her energy just about drained as she could see a place of refuge, a moment of rest ahead of them. The many times she had put her kids through hell flashed through her mind in the instant that the church door opened.

"Oh, hello," a young man said, taken aback, to see them standing there, wet, cold and shivering. "Come in, come in," he said, opening the door all the way and stepping aside so they could enter.

"We are not…" Patricia began, but he interrupted her.

"Pastor, do we have some towels and blankets in the back?" he called out, as he ushered them into the warmth of the building. "Come on in, it's warmer up here, away from the door," he said. "I will be right back." He scooted out a side door into a hallway and disappeared.

"What IS this place?" Kandy asked, looking around the room, possibly the largest room she had ever been in.

"This is a church," Patricia said, collapsing into a pew, sorry to be getting the seat so wet – but she was so drained, she could not stay on her feet for even another second. She kept Lesly on her lap as Kandy and Lonny clung tightly to each other.

"Good afternoon, young lady," a man said, coming into the room with an arm load of towels. "I'm Pastor Stronghart. That is some mighty strong weather out there. Here, let's get you all dry." He handed a towel to Patricia – a big, clean, fluffy towel – and wrapped one around Kandy and another one around Lonny.

"Thank you," Patricia said, remembering her manners,

as she cuddled Lesly and herself in the nice, warm, fresh-smelling towel.

"I'm Jason," the young man said, returning with a bundle of blankets. "We have some dry clothes for your kids to change into, if you want."

Patricia just stared at the two men, wondering what she would have to do for them.

"Here's another towel for your hair," the pastor said, holding a small pink towel out to her.

"Mommy, is this heaven?" Kandy asked.

Patricia was embarrassed. "No, no, this is not heaven," she said, aware of how close to heaven-like this place was, compared with most of the places she had taken her children. She avoided looking at the men, busying herself with drying her children. She could not allow herself to break down. They would get dry, the storm would stop, and she would get these kids to her mother's place. Those were the facts. She would not be sidetracked by her emotions or any church things that were going on here. She had to stick to her plan, now that she finally had a plan.

"Do you like hot dogs?" the pastor asked. "I was just about to fix a couple of hot dogs in the kitchen, and I could make some for you, too, if you like."

"Yes!" Kandy and Lonny shouted together.

Patricia knew this was going to cost her something, but she also knew her kids had not had anything to eat today, or yesterday, or, when had they eaten? Since she couldn't remember, she knew it was too long ago.

"Is it all right if they have a hot dog, Mom?" the pastor asked.

Patricia realized she had not yet introduced herself. "My name is Patricia, and this is Kandy, Lesly, and Lonny, and yes, they can have a hot dog." She dared not ask for one for herself, but she figured she could probably get a bite from each of theirs. Her stomach betrayed her by growling loudly.

"Do you want a hot dog, Sister Patricia?" the pastor said, surprising her. Why was he calling her 'sister'? She couldn't remember his name, but the other man, the younger man was named... hmmm... what was his name again? Well, it didn't matter. She would probably never see them again after today.

"Oh, no, that's okay," she said, looking at the floor. She did not really need food to exist. She had gone days and days without it before, even though the thought of eating a hot dog sounded, well, heavenly.

"Oh, sure, she wants one," the young man said, "and I would like one, too, Pastor."

"Come on, let's go back to the kitchen," the pastor said, leading the way. "Oh, if you want to change your children into dry clothes, the ladies' room is right there, and it has plenty of room for changing. Brother Jason, grab the bag of clothes and let's get these kids dry and warm."

Patricia followed the two men with her kids trailing behind her. Jason, this young man was named Jason. He was cleaner than most of the guys she knew. If he weren't so young, could he be interested in someone like her? No, no way, he was a Christian, and she was a... what was she? She was a free-thinker. She was an embracer of the new morality. She was a person who enjoyed mind-expanding experiences. Maybe, if he had money, he could help her out, just a little, after they had something to eat. Even a hot dog seemed like a gourmet meal to her at this moment.

She found some clothes that would fit Kandy and Lonny, but the ones she found for Lesly were either too big or too small. She had the kids use the bathroom, then she put a little pair of bulky pants on Lesly with a sweatshirt that was too big, but at least they were warm and dry. The thin rags her children had been wearing were not worth keeping, so she dropped them into the trash can. None of the clothes were even near her own size, so she dried herself the best she could and then wrapped up in a blanket. They couldn't do anything about their soaked shoes, so they just left them in the bathroom and walked to the church kitchen in clean, dry stocking feet, except for Patricia, who had no socks.

The smell of food cooking made her stomach turn. She shoved her kids into the kitchen and returned as quickly as she could to the bathroom and got sick in the toilet. This was why she didn't like to eat, or even to smell food, because her stomach didn't accept food. She began to shudder, needing something else. Maybe she could leave her kids here to eat while she went over to Nobby's – he was just a few blocks away from here – and maybe he would let her have just a little something to settle her stomach, something to get her through, until she could borrow a few dollars from her mother.

That thought calmed her shaky nerves, and she began to scheme on how she could make this happen. She could operate so much better without food upsetting her stomach, and with her brain cleared with some good stuff, even just a little, just a tiny bit, just enough...

"Sister Patricia, are you okay in there?"

The voice of Jason interrupted her plan, and she began to panic. Here she was, in a church bathroom, trying to figure something out, and this man that she didn't even know was intruding on her thoughts.

"Yeah," she called weakly, trying desperately to think of a way out. The bathroom window was high and tiny, too small for her to squeeze out of. If she could get this guy to go back to the kitchen, she could slip out the front door. The other man was a pastor – he would surely take care of her kids for a few minutes, until she got back.

"Do you need me to get you anything?" Jason called through the door.

Did she need him to get her anything? Of course she did! But it wasn't anything he could get for her. Maybe he could lend her some money. Yes, now there was a plan, the beginning of a plan. She didn't need much. Nobby would take a little as a down payment until she could get more.

She wiped her face on the towel and prepared to face this Jason guy. She opened the bathroom door. He was standing across the hall, looking very concerned.

"Do you think you could loan me a little cash?" she asked quietly, glancing down the hall to be sure the pastor couldn't hear her.

"Oh, sorry, man, I just started working yesterday," he said, turning up his empty palms to her, as if to show how empty they really were.

"Just a little?" she begged, against her own wishes. "A few bucks?"

"I don't have one brown penny on me," he said, shaking his head. "Sorry."

"Does the church have money for people in need?" she asked, a sudden brainstorm hitting her.

"You would have to ask Pastor about that," Jason said. "Come on back and get your hot dog and you can ask him."

She grabbed his sleeve. "Maybe you can ask him for me," she whispered.

"No, I don't think so," he said, looking into her eyes.

She violently let go of his sleeve. She knew his kind. He thought he was better than she was, because he was a holy-headed Christian. Well, she didn't need him to help her anyway. If he really was a Christian, he would just give her the money she needed and not make her play games with the pastor.

## Pastor Stronghart

"Here you go, Lonny," Pastor Stronghart said, smiling, putting a plate on the table in front of the little boy. The three children looked at him expectantly as he put a handful of potato chips on each plate. "I also have some baked beans in here. Do you like beans?"

"Yah!" they answered him.

"Let's say a prayer, and then you can go ahead and eat," he said, as Brother Jason came back into the kitchen.

"Is Mommy all right?" the little girl, Kandy, asked, looking at Brother Jason expectantly.

"She is," Brother Jason answered. "Go ahead with the prayer, Pastor."

"Father, in the precious name of Jesus, we thank You for these young people who are in our midst today. We ask that You bless them with what they need, take them safely where they need to go, and bless their mother. Bless this food as nourishment for our bodies. We love You, we praise You, and we thank You. In Jesus' name we pray. Amen."

"Can we eat now?" Kandy asked, poised to begin.

"You may begin," Pastor Stronghart said. He turned to the stove and grabbed the pan that held the baked beans. He put a spoonful on each of the plates. "Lonny! Where is your hot dog?"

Through a stuffed mouth, the little boy answered, "Here," as he pointed to his mouth.

These children seemed to be starving, and their mother

obviously had problems of her own. She didn't return to the kitchen before the food disappeared from their plates. Pastor Stronghart wasn't sure about giving them another hot dog – if they hadn't eaten in a long while, another hot dog could make them sick. He poured each of them a cup of milk, which they drank so quickly, he almost thought he had set empty cups in front of them. He decided to give each of them another half of a hot dog.

"Where is Mommy?" Kandy asked.

That was what Pastor Stronghart was just wondering. He looked at Brother Jason, who nodded and slipped out of the kitchen. He was back a moment later, and shook his head, shrugged his shoulders.

"Pastor, I have to leave in a few minutes so I can get to work on time," Brother Jason said. "This week I work swing shift, but starting next week I go in at four in the morning to unload the trucks. My bus comes by on 33rd in fifteen minutes."

Pastor Stronghart had planned to give Brother Jason a ride to work on his way to meet Brother William for another counseling session. Now he would have to change his plans, to accommodate these children. Their mother – he assumed she was their mother, anyway – had left them here, and he did not know if or when she was coming back to get them. He did not know their last name or where they lived. He could not take them with him – that might be considered kidnapping, even if he did have three car seats in his car, which he did not – and he could not call anyone to come and stay with them, since nobody knew them. He had no option but to stay here with them and see what miracle the Lord had in store for them today.

At times like this, only God could come through, because there was no other option.

## Officer Shotgun

The day was dark and stormy, but finally Officer Shotgun had another chance to go by that den of thieves, that church where he was going to catch them in the act of doing something illegal. He pulled into the parking lot across the street from the church and prepared to go inside the building. He was just about to open the car door when someone came out of the front door of the church. That woman was a drug addict. He didn't know her, but he knew by looking at her, the way she was so under-dressed for the weather, with bare feet, and the nervous way she was looking back and forth, up and down the street. From the way she was moving, he could tell she must be holding, and she must have gotten it from the dealer inside the church. Maybe if he got in there right away, he could catch them in the act, before they hid it or got it put away. She was just a user, small potatoes, not worth even following. The dealer must be still inside.

He waited until she ran down the street and then he secured his car. He ducked his head against the rain as he dashed across the street, but, even with his hat and coat on, he found himself drenched by the time he walked up the church steps. He opened the door, stepped inside, and found himself in an atmosphere that seemed like a different world. It felt so quiet and calm in here – they had to be pumping some kind of relaxant through the ventilator system.

"Hello?" he called out, though not too loudly. This place did not seem like a place to shout. He had to remember why he was here. He felt slightly disoriented and very uncomfortable. He thought he heard voices coming from another room, so he followed the sound to find the people. He hoped he would come upon them as they were making a transaction.

As he walked down the hallway, he saw a light shining from a room at the end of the hall. He slowed his pace, trying to pick up on the conversation.

"I wish I could help you out, Pastor," he heard a man's voice say, "but I have to take off now or I'm going to be late for my job."

"I'll just have to wait here, I suppose, and watch over these little darlings until she returns," another voice said.

That was it, Officer Shotgun thought. One guy was watching over 'little darlings,' one of the street names for drugs, until a user came to pick them up, and another guy was going 'do his job,' which meant he was about to deliver a stash to someone who was waiting. Officer Shotgun slipped into the men's room before he could be seen. He had to catch them in the act. If he just walked in on them with the drugs on the table, he could only get them for possession, not for dealing, which they were obviously doing, right here, using the church as a front. Why else would a church be open on a Wednesday afternoon? Why else would an addict be running away, and a so-called pastor be watching over 'little darlings?' Why else would the parking lot in this neighborhood be full of expensive cars on Sundays? They had to be dealing drugs here, and he was going to catch them.

He heard footsteps go by the door where he was hiding and waited a few more minutes. He didn't hear any other activity, so he finally decided this was not the time to catch them in the act. He had to get more evidence, he had to catch them at the moment they were making the deal. He quietly left the men's room and went out the front door of the church. He didn't see anyone coming, so he returned to his car.

He was not giving up on this! He would find out exactly what was going on, and he would be right there when the deal was made.

## Patricia

Patricia was so mad! That stupid Nobby would not open his door! She knew he was inside, and she needed a fix, she really needed one, right now! She ran around to the back door, but it was locked, too! He was just holding out on her, and he had no right to do that. He was her friend, was he not? She had been coming to him for more than a year, he had always been there for her, and now he was just stiffing her!

As she backed away from the front porch, she glanced around the neighborhood. She didn't see anyone else outside, and she did not know anyone who lived around here. She would have to go back to that church and get her kids. She smiled to herself when she remembered Kandy had called it a lighthouse. Poor kid, didn't even know what a church was.

Patricia turned the corner and was just two blocks away from the church when she saw a policeman come out the front door. What was he doing there? He must have been looking for her. She ducked behind a tree – it was slightly less wet under the leaves, but she became aware that the ground was poking her bare feet – until he crossed the street. She waited and watched as he drove away. He had not taken her kids with him, but was one of those social workers there, to take them away? Would that pastor do that to her? Oh, everyone was against her today! She could not get a break!

As soon as the cop was out of sight, she began to run back to the church. She paused for a moment outside the door, so she could catch her breath, then she eased the door open and tiptoed inside. As soon as she got near the ladies' room she began to walk normally, back to the kitchen.

"Are you ready to go?" she asked her kids, not looking the pastor in the eye. That other man, the younger one, was not in the kitchen.

"Hot dog," Lonny said.

"You had a hot dog, yes," Patricia said, nodding.

"More!" he shouted.

"No, you don't need another hot dog," she said firmly. She had to get them out of here right away, before some stupid social worker showed up and started asking questions.

"Are you okay, Sister Patricia?" the pastor asked.

"Yeah, sure," she said. "I was just in the bathroom. The hot dog didn't agree with me, I guess."

"I guess not," he said.

She did not look at him, because he was probably one of those people who could tell you were lying just by looking at you, so she didn't give him the chance.

"Come on, we need to get going," Patricia insisted.

"I want stay here," Kandy said. "Warm here."

"We will be warm when we get to Grandma's house," Patricia said, although she was not sure exactly how far away her mother's apartment was. She did know the general direction, though.

"Can I give you a lift?" the pastor asked. "I don't have any car seats in my car, though."

"Oh, no, thanks," Patricia said, "thanks anyway, but we don't need a ride." She was starting to form another plan in her mind. Otto lived not far from here, and she was sure they could crash there. Why hadn't she thought of him before? He wouldn't have any stuff, but he did have a house and two couches in the living room.

"Are you sure?" the pastor asked. "It would be no trouble at all."

"We just have a couple more blocks to go," Patricia said, grabbing Lesly so she could carry her, "but thanks again. Come on, kids, let's go! We are almost there!"

"Well, Sister Patricia, you are welcome to come back any time, and bring your children, too. Have they been dedicated to the Lord yet?"

She had to hold back a laugh. What did that even mean? They had never even been inside a church before! They had thought this was a lighthouse!

"No," she said, embarrassed to tell the pastor that she had no idea what he was talking about.

"You need to do that," he said. "Come back on Sunday and we can talk about it."

"Oh, yeah, sure," she said, with absolutely no intention of following through on that one. She gathered up her children and herded them toward the door.

"It was nice meeting you," the pastor said.

"Yeah, you too," Patricia answered, hoping, for her children's sake, that the rain had let up. She glanced down at her bare feet but did not want to retrieve her soggy shoes from the bathroom. They were barely more than a few threads attached to a sole, anyway.

"Are you sure I can't give you a ride?" he asked again.

"No, that's okay, we will be fine," she answered. She didn't need his help. They were always fine.

## Evelyn

With her Bible Studies course and her Bible on the table in front of her, Evelyn began to read. She glanced up at the clock, to be sure she would study for at least thirty minutes. She would like to say she would study for one hour per day, but she did not want to commit to something she could not do. She wondered how long it would take to go through the entire course? Would it take a whole year? This was just one lesson – did Pastor Stronghart say this was the first month's study lesson?

She began to examine her Bible before she started on the lesson. Her Bible was new-looking, only having been opened in church for those years when she had been taking her daughter. She looked at the table of contents: sixty-six books in the Bible, the Book of books, it was called. She began to read the introduction – a very nice, thorough introduction, right in the front of her Bible, she discovered, with guidelines for studying the Bible. When she finished, she began to explore the rest of her Bible. At the back were ten pages of color maps – the Bible in the time of Genesis, the Exodus from Egypt, Jerusalem at the time of Jesus, Paul's journeys, to name a few.

She turned to the book of Genesis, the first book in the Bible, where her study course started. She wondered if that other lady – Carolina, was that her name? – was starting on her course yet. Well, no matter, Evelyn was determined to keep up with her studying. It actually was very intriguing already. She reviewed the outline for Genesis and then she read the first chapter. She read the notes for the chapter, then she went on to chapter two, the outline, the chapter and then the notes. She was about to start on chapter three when she happened to look at the clock. What? More than two hours had gone by already? And this was really getting interesting!

More than two hours had passed and she had not once thought of Marilyn. Evelyn was really feeling very good. She would get something to eat, then come back and study chapter three. She found herself thinking about the Bible and some of the insights provided by the notes and outlines, instead of feeling sorry for herself.

Perhaps reading the Bible was exactly what she needed!

## William

William Dorsett waited for Pastor Stronghart to arrive. Today they were meeting at the library, in a back corner. When they had gone to the coffee shop last time they met, the place was so crowded that William didn't have a chance to tell his pastor what was going on. Now, only one other man was here – another brother, much darker than William – dressed in a suit, all fancy with a vest and tie and everything. He could almost be another preacher. He was intently reading one of those big, thick books that they didn't let you take out of the library, had his nose so far into it, the book could have been attached to his face.

William turned his attention to Pastor Stronghart, who was now approaching.

"Hey, Brother William, I see you made it," Pastor Stronghart said, reaching over to give him a hug.

It felt nice, the human touch, William thought. "Yeah, I got here early," he said.

"You are looking good," Pastor Stronghart said encouragingly.

"Thanks, Pastor," William said, wondering where to start.

"This is the day the Lord has made. Let us rejoice and be glad in it."

William tried to give him a smile. He could feel his pastor looking at him, but he could not meet his eyes.

"So, what is going on?" Pastor Stronghart asked. "God is still in the blessing business. Why are you looking so down?"

William glanced around the library, looking for a better answer among the books. He wished that other guy would leave so they would have more privacy. This area was very secluded, but that guy was just sitting there, acting like he was reading. He would probably be able to hear everything they said at this table. Well, William was desperate. He needed help now, and Pastor Stronghart was the only person he could trust.

"Pastor Stronghart, I just have to tell you, and I don't know how to say it," William began. "See, well, you know my mom died a few months ago."

"Yes, Son, I did her funeral," Pastor Stronghart reminded him.

"Yeah, I know, I mean, well, Mom took care of all of our finances," William said. "We had the house and I thought it was all paid for, and I didn't know she took out a loan on the house so she could keep paying the other bills while she was still alive. All this was happening automatically, from the bank to the utility places, and I still haven't figured it all out. But the thing is, somehow, they had it set up so when she died, either all the balance would have to be paid or they would get the house. Pastor Stronghart, they are going to take the house away from me, my mom's house, where I have lived my whole life." He was so mad at those thieves who tricked his mom that he could spit, but he was also so upset that he might start to cry at any second.

"But I was there when the lawyer drew up her will, and she left the house to you," Pastor Stronghart said. "One thing she clearly stated was that she wanted take care of you, since you gave up everything to take care of her."

"Yeah, I know, but I got these guys coming by the house, and they gave me this contract, and, you know, I am no mathematical genius or anything, but to me, it looks likes they are telling the truth, and it is her signature, I recognized it." William was sweating now. It had been so hard to get over losing his mom – he still wasn't really over it – and now he was going to lose her house, too.

"Don't let the devil make you worry unnecessarily," Pastor Stronghart said.

"I'm going to lose my mom's house!" William quietly shouted. "Where am I going to live? I do not have any resources. I don't have any family. Mom was an only child, my dad was an only child, and I am an only child. You know what that means, don't you? I don't have any aunts and uncles, I don't have any cousins or brothers or sisters or anyone who can help me out!"

"How much do you owe on the house?" Pastor Stronghart asked.

"What difference does it make?" William shrugged, lowering his voice. "It could be two hundred dollars or two hundred thousand dollars and it wouldn't make any difference because I don't have it." He eyed that other guy, who seemed to be listening to what they were saying, but now, William didn't care. He just needed help, and he needed it yesterday.

"How much do you owe?" Pastor Stronghart repeated quietly. "Approximately?"

"I can't remember," William confessed. "I was going

to bring the paperwork and I forgot it at home. Every time I leave the house, I am afraid when I get back the locks will be changed, with a notice that it isn't my house any more. I sneaked out the back door, just in case they were watching."

"We need to know the amount, so we can pray about it," Pastor Stronghart said.

"Why?" William said. "God already knows the amount."

"We want to be specific in our prayers," Pastor Stronghart explained. "We don't just go to God and say, 'bless the world.' We go to Him with specifics. If you need one hundred thousand dollars, you ask Him for one hundred thousand dollars."

"Just like that," William said, snapping his fingers.

"No, I am not saying that God works like a magical genie," Pastor Stronghart said, "granting our every wish. You know that. Your mother raised you in the church. You know God better than that, don't you?"

"Yeah," William agreed, settling back in his chair a bit.

"God deals with specifics. He provides us with what we need, when we need it, not when we want it."

"Well, be sure to tell Him that I need it right now," William said. "If He waits too long, it will be too late."

"If that happens, that means that God has another plan for you," Pastor Stronghart said. "You just have to trust Him."

"How can I, when my finances are so messed up? Since Mom died, I don't have any income."

"Hasn't God brought you this far?" Pastor Stronghart asked, looking straight into William's eyes.

"I guess so," William said, looking down at the table.

"What do you mean, 'I guess so?' Of course He has. And He has not brought you this far to leave you," Pastor Stronghart assured him.

Suddenly William had a thought, a hope. "Does the church have a fund for something like this? I could pay you back." He didn't know how, but he would find a way, if only he could save his mom's house.

"Our Benevolence Fund would not be able to help you, since we have just about $42 in it," Pastor Stronghart said.

William's hopes fell. He didn't know why he had thought Pastor Stronghart could help him. This had been his last hope, and now, this was it. He was going to lose his mom's house for sure.

"Brother William, there are programs in place to help prevent you from losing your house," Pastor Stronghart said.

"What do you mean? What kind of programs?" He had never heard about anything like this.

"Oh, yes, indeed, President Obama put all kinds of programs in place to help homeowners keep their homes."

"Are you serious?" William asked, glad that he had voted for once in his life, for President Obama.

"Excuse me," the man at the other table said, rising from his seat. "I hope you don't mind, but I couldn't help but overhear what you have been discussing."

Oh, great, William thought, now even this guy knew his business.

"I'm Pastor Stronghart," his pastor said, standing to shake hands.

"Very nice to meet you, Pastor Stronghart. My name is Decca Minor," the man said, shaking hands with each of them.

"William Dorsett," William said, motioning for Decca Minor to take a seat.

They all sat at the table. William looked at Mr. Minor expectantly.

"Do you wonder who I am?" Mr. Minor asked, then he proceeded to answer his own question. "Of course you do. Can I help you with your seemingly impossible situation? Yes, indeed, I certainly can. How can I help you? I work for Shirelles Mortgage Relief," he said with a smile. "What is Shirelles Mortgage Relief? We are a non-profit government-sponsored organization. What do we do? We help people who are in danger of losing their homes."

"But I owe around eighty thousand dollars, or something like that, and the amount grows every day," William said.

"The amount you owe makes absolutely no difference," Mr. Minor said reassuringly. "You could owe two thousand dollars or you could owe five hundred thousand dollars, but either way, you can depend on us. We can help you. What will we do first? We can look at the contract, and see if it is legitimate. What will we do next? Depending on what your contract says, we can go from there."

"How much is this going to cost me?" William asked. "Because I am flat broke, with no income."

"That is a very good question, and I am glad you asked me that. Our services will not cost you a dime," Decca Minor said, "and if we find that you have been taken advantage of, or if they took advantage of your mom, we can go after them and get a settlement for you."

"And you get part of that, right?" William said. He knew this guy had to get something from him.

"Oh, no, oh, no, we won't get a penny out of your settlement," Mr. Minor answered, shaking his head dramatically.

"How can this be?" William asked. "Nothing is free."

"We get paid by a government grant," Decca Minor said, holding up one finger to make his point.

William could tell Mr. Minor was getting paid very well, by the way he dressed.

"Here is my card. My office is just across the block, in the bright yellow building with the red trim. Come and see me and I'll see what we can do. All you have to do is come and I can guarantee we can help you, one way or another, so you won't lose your house." Decca Minor stood and did a little bow.

"Pastor Stronghart, William, it was nice to meet you. You know, I am glad I decided to spend my lunch hour in the library today."

"So are we, Mr. Minor," Pastor Stronghart said, standing to shake his hand again. "Thank you so much.

You are an answer to a prayer."

"And we didn't even pray yet!" William said, also standing.

"God said, 'before you ask, I will answer,' and He just proved it again," Pastor Stronghart said. "Isaiah 65:24 says, 'Before they call I will answer; while they are still speaking I will hear,' and that's the Word."

"God said it, I believe it, and that settles it," William said, reciting a quote he had learned in Sunday School years ago.

"Amen, Brother William," Pastor Stronghart said.

"I will see you at my office," Decca Minor said. "You don't need an appointment, just ask for me."

"Thank you, Mr. Minor," William said, a bit of his burden beginning to lighten.

"And there is your miracle, Brother William," Pastor Stronghart said.

"I think you are right, Pastor," he said, nodding. Now he had real hope.

## Carolina

Carolina was sitting in her favorite chair - the only chair she could sit in comfortably and get out of easily. She glanced across the room at the photograph that had been taken at her graduation from nursing school, the young, slender, beautiful girl in the nursing cap.

How had she gotten from there to here? She had only gained about one pound per month - she had kept a journal - but who would have thought, year after year, she would just keep gaining? She had thought that at one point, she would have hit a plateau. Well, now, perhaps she had reached that plateau, after gaining more than 200 pounds.

She had set her Bible study notes on the kitchen table. She would need to catch a nap before she could even think about studying. She would also need to find her Bible. In the course introduction, which she had briefly read, part of each study lesson was to read the Bible. She had a Bible, somewhere, maybe it was in her bedroom, or maybe it was in her little sewing room? She would find it later, after she got a little rest. She was so tired right now.

## Jason

Jason moved into position to unload the cart onto the shelf. He felt like he was glowing with happiness - God was so good to him. He did not deserve it, but God was so very good. Look at him, here, working, while so many other people were still out there, trying to find a job.

A young girl who looked to be about fifteen years old came up beside him and started helping him put the items on the shelf.

"So, you are new here?" she asked. She showed him her name tag. "I'm Anita Bacon, I have been here for almost one month. What is your name?"

"Your name is Anita Bacon?" he asked, thinking how much it sounded like Anita Baker.

"That is MY name," she said, giggling. "What's yours?"

"I'm Jason," he said.

"Jason! Oh, that is such a nice name!" she squealed. "Your mom must have known how you were going to turn out."

"What do you mean?" he asked, confused.

"Well, just look at you!" Anita squeaked. "You can be nothing less than a Jason! So, how do you like it here?" She stopped working and sat on the edge of the cart so she could talk without interruption.

"It's great," he began, before she took over the conversation. He kept unloading the cart as she talked.

"You know, Jason, that name is so much like Jackson,"

she said. "And do you ever wonder why we never see Michael Jackson and Janet Jackson together, at the same time?"

"Could it be because Michael Jackson is dead?" Jason asked, stifling a laugh.

"No, silly, I mean, before!" she said, examining her fingernails.

"Um, no," he answered.

"I know all about the conspiracy," she said, lowering her voice.

"The conspiracy?" he asked, raising one eyebrow. Anita seemed to be kind of wacky, but as long as he was working, that was the important thing.

"The truth is, there was only one," she said quietly, looking up and down the aisle.

"Only one what?" he asked, as he continued to stock the shelf

She looked around to be sure no one else was listening. "They were one and the same."

"They were?" he asked, humoring her.

"There was only one of them," she said, as if that explained it all.

"Only one?" he asked.

"Michael Jackson was really Janet Jackson!" she said. "That is why you never saw them together! Janet Jackson stepped into her alter ego - which was Michael Jackson - and after he became a big hit, and she got rich, then she could be herself."

"You know, I think I did see them together, on TV," he said.

"Yeah, but that was after 2000, right? When they didn't look alike anymore? They got someone else to stand in for him, and someone else was the one who died. Don't you see? It is so obvious, when you know the hidden facts! Janet Jackson didn't want to keep on playing the game. After her 2004 'wardrobe malfunction,' she was a big enough star so that she no longer needed her alter ego. So a different guy, one who didn't even look like her at all, died, and she said it was her brother, Michael Jackson, and then she was free."

"But what about –" he began.

"Miss Bacon, shouldn't you be back in the back, loading up carts?" a young man said, probably a few years younger than Jason. He had on a name tag that said "Dole Bundon - Assistant Manager."

"I just wanted to make our new employee feel welcome," she said, pouting, getting up from her seat on the cart. She stomped her feet a couple of times on her way to the back.

"Welcome, Jason," Mr. Bundon said.

"Thank you, sir," he responded.

"I hope you don't think you can spend all your time here talking to the other employees," Dole said.

"No, sir," Jason said, continuing to work.

"And one other thing," Dole said, leaning into Jason, breathing in his face. "I heard that you are a Christian. This is a workplace. You do your job here. I don't want you talking to other employees about God or Jesus. I don't want you talking to any customers about Jesus. I don't want you to say the name of Jesus at any time while you are here, and especially not to customers. I don't want you wearing any kind of those coded Christian symbols on your clothing or on your ears or tattooed on your arms. I don't want you talking about your holy-roller experiences or talking in funny languages or doing any kind of your Christian hokey-pokey or hocus-pocus, trying to hypnotize people or anything. I don't want to see any kind of Christian literature or any posters of Jesus, and don't try making any displays into the shape of the cross. And no Christian music, no singing and no humming and no whistling of Christian tunes is allowed anywhere in this store, not in the back, and certainly, not in the front.

"Do you understand me, Jason?" he asked, stepping back and smiling.

"Yes, sir," Jason replied, wondering where all his hostility was coming from.

"Then you and I will get along just fine," Dole Bundon said, turning on his heels and walking away.

## Pastor Stronghart

Pastor Stronghart sat in his office, reviewing the church financial records. The church had not had a treasurer for a couple of months, and the records seemed to be sparse, until he took a closer look. He wasn't a math wiz, but the records seemed to be complete, with entries made every week – it was just that the finances were low, very low. In the record of the tithers, he and his wife were the only ones who contributed regularly one-tenth of their income, unless other members only grossed twenty to fifty dollars each month. One time a church member, who was not even a tither, asked if he should tithe on his gross income or on his net income, and the answer that the Lord instantly gave Pastor Stronghart was, "Do you want God to bless your gross income, or your net income?" That member never returned to Total Missionary Baptist Church after that.

As he compared the church offerings with the bills, Pastor Stronghart was amazed - again - at how God had brought in the exact amount needed every month, and no bill was unpaid or behind in its payment. He began to praise and worship God all by himself, as he asked for guidance on who could possibly be the next church treasurer. It would have to be a regular member with a mind for numbers. That cut down his options considerably, but he was confident that God would show him soon who this new treasurer would be.

He mentally listed the stops he had to make before he could call it a day. First, he was going to visit Mother Jonnigan in the nursing home. She was ninety-four now and she had been a faithful member of the church until she had to go into assisted living. She was always so happy to see him. While he was there, he would check and see if Brother Joshua was still there – he had been admitted while recovering from a broken hip. He had only attended Total Missionary Baptist Church for a few months, but he was a member of the church, and he still needed encouragement. The next stop would be the hospital, where Sister Cherie had just had her baby boy. He had hoped to take his wife with him for this visit, but since the baby had come early in the day and he would be in the area anyway, he planned to stop in while he was there. The last stop he was planning was in that direction, but farther out. God had put it on his heart to check on Mother Watkins, whose brother had recently passed away back in New York, and she had not been able to go to his funeral.

He took one more look around the church to see if anything needed to be done. Everything looked good, so he started on his rounds with a  smile on his face. He loved everything about ministry.

## Cyrus

Cyrus Miles tried to roll onto his side by gripping the rail on his hospital bed, but it was no use. He didn't have the strength in his arms. He had called for the nurse a long time ago, but she was ignoring him. Meanwhile, he was suffering, in pain, stuck flat on his back. He needed help, but none was available to him.

He sighed as he stared at the ceiling. He could use a visitor. He was sick of watching TV and he was sick of hospital food. He was sick of being sick, but the doctors had not been able to give him any hope of recovery. He wanted to climb out of this bed, walk out of this hospital and never come back. He could just as easily be confined to his own bed at home while nothing was being done to help him, as he was here.

A commotion in the hallway got his attention, as people were laughing and talking. Cyrus turned his head to see what was happening. A black man with a huge smile on his face looked right at Cyrus. The joy on the man's face immediately turned to concern as he stepped boldly into the room.

"What are you?" Cyrus asked, curious about this unusual man.

"I am a Christian," the man replied. "My name is Pastor Stronghart."

"I want to talk to you," Cyrus said, inviting the pastor to his bedside. This was exactly what he needed! Now maybe he could get some answers from God.

## Shannon

Shannon heard the garage door open and ran to greet her husband. Although they had been married for more than twenty-five years, she still felt excited to see him. He was always busy helping people and she wanted to be a good helper to him, so he could do a better job, so he could have more to give. She did her best to make their home a sanctuary from the rest of the world: a place he could come and relax and get away from the multitude of spirits that were constantly bombarding him when he was out doing the Lord's work. When he came home, he could be recharged without being more drained than he already was. Although she worked outside of the home and was not home during the day, she also worked inside the home, making it the best possible home they could share.

"Good evening, Dear," she said, as he came through the door from the garage.

He greeted her with a kiss. He still made her feel beautiful every time he looked at her.

"Hello, my Darling," he said, wrapping one arm around her while holding his coat, his wallet and a large envelope in the other hand.

"How was your day?" she asked, walking with him into the kitchen.

"It was great, and it got even better when I smelled what you have cooking!" He took his things into the dining room and set them on the chair. "We had a great prayer meeting at noon today."

"I was praying along with you at noon, even though I couldn't be at the church," she said, peeking in on the lasagna that was cooking in the crock pot. Steam and a glorious scent escaped from the open lid.

"Thank you. We needed it," he said, sitting down to remove his shoes.

She pulled a pad and pen out of the drawer, sat across from him at the table, and asked, "Who do we need to put on our prayer list today?"

## Lorenzo

Lorenzo Roberto Williamson III left the employment office trying to not be discouraged. He kept his head down to avoid the stares of the other people who were hanging around the building. He should not be here. He had been working in the warehouse making good money at a big company for almost four years. Then one day, out the blue, the company shut down. He never did find out why the business had closed, but suddenly nearly three hundred people were out of work and competing for jobs in this town that had about three openings.

He had immediately joined a church, just like his grandmother down in Louisiana had taught him, to help pray him through his troubles. He had asked the congregation to pray for him and he had been going to church every Sunday, but God had not yet honored his faithfulness. Pastor Stronghart told him every week to keep his faith, to keep believing, to not lose his joy, but after these months of being unemployed, it was getting hard. He was only twenty-three years old, he was stronger and leaner than most men his age, and he had his high school diploma. Those were three things that he had going for him, three more things than many of his former co-workers had, but the few available jobs required even more qualifications than he had. He would take any kind of job, even flipping burgers, if that were the only position available, but in the weeks he had been coming here, there had not been one job available that he could do.

His unemployment checks wouldn't keep coming forever – and he was ashamed to be getting them anyway.

He needed to be working, or he was going to go crazy. He decided to walk home instead of taking the bus, to give him more time away from the house and away from his girlfriend, Conya.

He loved Conya, and he loved their little daughter, Ebony, but he could not stand the tension at home while he was unemployed. He had planned to propose to Conya before he had lost his job, but now things seemed to be falling apart. She was edgy, grumpy, constantly asking if he had looked at this place or that place or put in an application at this other place; or she was telling him about the employment success stories of other people she knew from the company.

"Hey, Brother," another brother called, as he crossed the street. Lorenzo nodded to him and tried to pass by him, but he blocked his path. Lorenzo stood up straight, revealing his entire height. He was not about to be robbed, even if he didn't have anything worth stealing.

"Hey, Brother," the guy said again, lowering his voice, "I know where you can get some really good stuff." He stayed in front of Lorenzo, walking backwards, as Lorenzo tried to walk by him.

"Not today," Lorenzo answered.

"Come on, you know you want it," he said, staying right in Lorenzo's face.

"No, thanks," Lorenzo said, turning on his heels to go the other way.

The guy ran around him, supercharged. "Sure you do. It will bring up your hung-down head, I guarantee you that."

"Look, man, I am flat broke," Lorenzo said.

"Then I can help you!" the guy said, really getting excited. "You help me get rid of some, and I give you a cut of the take. You can get rich today!"

"You gonna pay me today?" Lorenzo asked, with no intention of following through on this, but just to get the guy off his back. Maybe he should have taken the bus instead of walking home.

"Yeah, man, I got your number."

"You got my number?" Lorenzo asked, stopping in his tracks. "This is my number: three." He held up three fingers. "That's one for the Father, one for the Son, and one for the Holy Ghost. You got that number?"

"Hey, so, you are a Jesus Freak, that don't matter, man," the guy said. "What would Jesus do? He would help a brother out, man."

Lorenzo abruptly ran across the street, narrowly missing a passing car. The dealer guy did not follow him, so Lorenzo kept jogging until he got to the next bus stop. He could not let himself think about how easy it would be to make a living by dealing. He really needed to find a job, and he needed to do it right away.

## Chester

Chester Deacon finished changing the tire on his car and wiped his hands on a rag. Now he and his wife would be able to get to church on Sunday. They had an old Ford pickup truck, which was fine for him, but he did not want Sandra to have to ride in that old thing in her Sunday best. He worked every day to make her life comfortable. She was the love of his life.

He had known her all his life. They had grown up next door to each other in Portland, and when they were both eight years old, he asked her to marry him. She said yes, but they would have to wait until they were nine. He waited. She teased around with other boys, but was never serious with any of them. Sandra always came back to Chester. He told her they had been made for each other. He never had any interest in any other girl. He already knew the only one he wanted.

When she turned sixteen, he asked her parents for permission to marry their daughter, and they told him, if he really loved her, he could wait – so he kept waiting. The day she turned eighteen was the day they got married, so her birthday was also their anniversary, making it easy for him to remember that date. Actually, it would be impossible for him to forget, since she reminded him so often.

Chester was a romantic at heart, although he did not always know the best way to show it. He brought flowers when he thought about it, not just on special occasions, and he brought Sandra a stuffed teddy bear, one long-stemmed rose and a big box of chocolate candy every year on Valentine's Day. Their spare room was just about filled with teddy bears of every color and size. They had been married nearly thirty-five years, and when he looked at her, he still saw that little girl he had always loved. He indulged her when he could, even against the orders of her doctor. The doctor said she was diabetic and slightly overweight, but she looked so beautiful to Chester. He could not see anything wrong with her.

He wanted to surprise her with something special for their thirty-fifth anniversary, but he didn't yet know how he was going to do that. He checked the calendar and saw that her birthday was on a Sunday this year – this would be perfect! They could celebrate with the entire church family, at church. He knew the pastor and his family would organize a great dinner after Sunday morning worship service. He would have to call Pastor Stronghart and make plans – in secret – to surprise his wife on her birthday, their anniversary. She would not be suspicious if he took her out to buy a new Sunday dress, because he did that at least a couple times every year. Yes, this was going to be the best surprise birthday-anniversary celebration that anyone ever had, he was going to make sure of it.

## Officer Shotgun

Officer Shotgun was livid. The captain was transferring him to the other side of town, nearly at the edge of the county! Just when he was sure he was going to be able to catch that pastor in the act of dealing.

He had to admit, he had not been going by the books on this investigation. He had started it all on his hunch, because he knew nothing good could come out of a church. He had attended church, one of the mega-churches on his side of town, with his ex-wife while they were married, and he had seen all the hypocrites there. Everyone had gone there on Sundays to show off their expensive suits and fancy jewelry, to smile at all the people they actually hated, and to do their token good deeds by raising money for the poor people in other countries; but nobody really lived that kind of life. Some of the deacons at his church had been busted with prostitutes so many times, a fact only they and he, as the arresting officer, would know. Many of the members were out bar-hopping on Saturday nights and couldn't even stay awake at church. During Sunday service, he could still smell the alcohol on their breath. Other church officers were crooked in their business and the ones they called elders were the meanest, snootiest people in town, looking down their long noses at the rest of the people. Those elders would crack their faces if they ever cracked a smile, their lips were sealed so tight. The one hour they spent in church was all the torture they could take, and the parking lot would be completely empty in seconds flat. Most of them came to church for the eight o'clock service so their Sundays wouldn't be messed up. After nine, they had the whole day free.

Yes, he knew all about church people. There was no way anyone would come to church in the middle of the week unless they were getting something, and now he knew what they were getting at that little church in the city's drug neighborhood. The problem was, now he would be covering ground on the other side of the city from the church. He would not have a chance to happen by and catch them in the act. He had to come up with another plan, but right now, all he could do was to follow orders.

Well, as long as those criminals were committing crimes in this city, they were going to get caught, he would make sure of that, somehow. Yes, he would definitely make sure of that.

## Jason

The devil had seriously been trying to steal Jason's joy. His manager at work must have made an announcement that he was a Christian, and the other workers were constantly teasing him. "Do a miracle, Jesus Freak," and "Hallelujah, Holy Roller," were the greetings they used most often, before laughing and giggling at him. Jason knew God had given him this job, so he just smiled and did his work without complaining. The only One he could go to for help was the Lord Himself, and Jason was praying on the job all day long.

At home, the devil seemed to have taken control of his mom as well. She had started smoking again, even in the house, and she knew how much the smell of smoke bothered him. When he tried to talk to her, she replied with a snap. He offered to pray with her, and she threatened to kick him out of the house. After several days of being bombarded by satanic attacks, he had to call his pastor. As soon as he got home from work, he made sure his mother was not in the house and he dialed Pastor Stronghart's number.

"Praise the Lord!" Pastor Stronghart answered in a joyful voice.

How wonderful to hear somebody with a positive attitude!

"Hi, Pastor Stronghart," Jason said, trying to make his mood sound light.

"Brother Jason!" Pastor Stronghart said. "It's so good to hear from you. How are you doing on that job the Lord gave you?"

"I am so thankful, Pastor," he began, flopping down on the sofa. "I needed a job so badly and I do know the Lord opened the door for me, and I just walked right in. I have been there, what, three, four months now?"

"Do I detect a note of sadness in your voice, Brother Jason?" Pastor Stronghart asked.

"I'm not sure if it is sadness, exactly," he said, tracing the pattern on the sofa with his finger. "More like frustration, maybe, I think."

"And why would you be frustrated on a job that God gave you?"

"It's not the job that's the problem," he answered, not knowing how to bring up the subject.

"Are you having problems at home?" Pastor Stronghart asked.

"No, well, my mom kind of has a demonic spirit about her," he confessed, "but that is not why I am feeling frustrated."

"I will put your mother's name on my prayer list," Pastor Stronghart said. Jason knew he was writing down her name at that very moment. Pastor Stronghart did not wait to pray, he started praying for a person the moment he heard that he or she had a need.

"Thank you, Pastor, I appreciate that," Jason said, running his fingers through his hair. "She needs it. But the reason I called is because I am having a real situation with my co-workers at my job, and especially my manager. It was on, like, my first or second day on the job, and my manager came over to me and gave me a five-minute lecture on how he didn't want to hear me talking about

Jesus, or in any way showing my Christian faith. Isn't that the opposite from what Jesus said for us to do, when He told us to go into all the world, teaching all nations about the Gospel?"

"But when the door is shut, Brother Jason, we are not to try to force our way in," Pastor Stronghart said. "We are not going to win anyone to Christ if we try to beat them over the head with the Bible. People – non-Christians – look at our lives and see how we live. Now, how are you responding to your manager's orders? Are you being obedient, or are you trying to sneak around and disobey what he said, just for the sake of trying to speak up for Jesus?"

"No, Pastor, I am doing exactly what he said, because I can't lose this job. I need to work, and I don't want to give him any reason to fire me."

"And how are you doing on your job?" Pastor Stronghart asked.

"I am getting all my work done, every day, even though all my co-workers are taunting me and calling me a Jesus Freak or Holy Roller. I don't really talk to them. I mean, I am friendly, and I try to stay joyful, but I don't really get into any conversation with them. I just concentrate on my work."

"Good! That is exactly what you should be doing. That is the best way you can witness: by being a good worker, an honest worker, and not wasting your time talking and gossiping. People look at you and they see a man who has a good work ethic, who gets to work on time, who is there to get the job done, and then they discover you are a Christian. Some day, someone will come up to you, maybe outside of work, and ask you how you do it, how you keep your joy when all these forces seem to be piling up against you. What are you going to say when they ask you that?"

"I will just tell them the truth," Jason began, holding one finger up in the air, the finger of truth.

"The truth is always the best answer," Pastor Stronghart agreed.

"I will tell them that I could only do my job the way I am doing it, with joy, with Jesus right alongside me, every minute."

"Praise God!" Pastor Stronghart shouted.

"Is God testing me?" Jason asked.

"I do not think God tests us in this way," Pastor Stronghart said. "This is more like the way the devil works, trying every way he can to get our minds off the Lord, to throw our lives off track. The devil knows you are a good witness for Christ, and that is damaging to his work, trying to lure ones away from God. He has so many weapons, and a good one he is using today is by keeping people too busy to think about God.

"Even in some of the churches, people are so busy with committees and meetings and trying to organize ways to help the poor – now, don't get me wrong, I have nothing against helping the poor – but people are so busy between their jobs and their families and their sporting events and keeping up with their television programs, their computer programs and email, they have no time left to come to church and to study the Word of God. People are trying to fill their lives with every little detail, not realizing they are missing the one most important detail – Jesus Christ in their lives."

"Will you put my manager's name on your prayer list?" Jason asked. "His name is Dole Bundon."

"Dole, like the pineapple?" Pastor Stronghart asked.

"Yeah, like pineapple," Jason laughed. He had not thought about that before.

"And what was that last name again?"

"Bundon: B-U-N-D-O-N," Jason spelled for him.

"Dole Bundon, got it," Pastor Stronghart said. "You know, I think I know his mother. I will pray for both of them."

"He is really anti-Christian," Jason added.

"Brother Jason, let me tell you what happened to me on a job that I once had," Pastor Stronghart said. Jason loved his pastor's stories about his life of faith because they were so encouraging. He settled into the couch to listen, the phone pressed against his ear.

"I was called into my supervisor's office on my first day on the job. My supervisor, who was a woman, and a man who was a supervisor in another department were sitting there, in the only two chairs. I looked around for a place to sit, but there weren't any other chairs in the little office, so I just stood there. They knew I was a minister, and they really went after me, one after the other. 'You better not do any preaching on the job,' one said, then the other said, 'and don't even mention anything about Jesus to anybody, ever.' The other one said, 'don't bring any religious literature into the building,' and the other one said, 'don't try to recruit people to come to your church.' They went on for about ten minutes, telling me all the things I was not allowed to do, including putting a Christmas tree in my office or playing Christmas carols on the CD player. I was much like you, in that I agreed with what they were telling me to do, since, like you, I needed the job. But I was praying. I was asking the Lord to take control of the situation, and if He would open a door, no matter what they said, I would share the Gospel.

"I started working, and, like you, I just did my job the best way I could. I was working as unto the Lord, knowing He is my real supervisor. I was friendly to the other employees, and they knew I was a minister, but I didn't force my beliefs on anyone. I kept doing my job, and I kept praying.

"Well, after I had worked there for a little more than a year, one morning I came into work, and the whole atmosphere had changed." He let out a little laugh.

"What do you mean?" Jason asked. "Changed how?"

"That morning, there were crosses all over the place, and all these signs that said, 'What Would Jesus Do?' and Christian music was playing over the sound system. On the file cabinets were Christian magnets, and there were posters on the walls with Christian sayings on them. At first, I was thinking that I had been set up, that someone had plastered these things all over to blame me. My supervisor called me into her office, and there she was, with the other supervisor, and she announced, 'We just became Christians! We both got saved last night at a revival!' And they really went overboard, taking over the whole office with everything Christian."

"No kidding?" Jason asked, although he knew his

pastor was not one to kid.

"They became Christians and they had prayer every morning at work, and then they ended up getting married and I performed the wedding ceremony. They still go to one of the churches across town."

"That is amazing," Jason said, smiling and nodding.

"That is the amazing power of prayer," Pastor Stronghart added.

## Carolina

Carolina was slightly ashamed of herself. She had been going to the church for a few months, and she had an improved attitude about life, but she was having a hard time getting going on the Bible studies lessons. She had not even finished the first month's lessons. That other lady, Evelyn, the one she had met the first time she had gone to Total Missionary Baptist Church, was keeping up and doing her lessons every day. Carolina knew this because Evelyn was always announcing how happy she was, even though her daughter had not yet come home from college for a visit. Evelyn said she was so much more fulfilled because of the Word of God. Carolina still did not see how that could make much of a difference, but she did really want to know. She was going to have to find a way to be motivated.

What was Pastor Stronghart often saying was so important when studying the Bible? Oh, yes, he said to always start with prayer. She had been listening to other people pray at church, but she didn't really practice it on her own. Maybe she should start. She needed to do something to get moving in this area. She had always been a good student and prompt at finishing her homework, but now she kept finding excuses not to do it: the lesson was way over on the table and she didn't want to get up; she was going to start, but she left her Bible in her bedroom; she forgot all about it some days; she didn't want to start before one of her favorite shows was coming on TV, because she might get too involved and then miss her program.

She was hungry now, so she got up and walked to the refrigerator. Strange, it was so easy to get up out of her chair when it involved food, yet so hard when the idea of studying the Bible was in her mind.

Suddenly she had a brainstorm! She would put the lessons in the refrigerator! Then, every time she got up to get something to eat, she would see the Bible Studies lesson, and she would have to do the lesson before she could have a meal or a snack! And she would start this new method right now.

## Lorenzo

It was only eleven o'clock in the morning on a Wednesday, but Lorenzo was already waiting for Pastor Stronghart to open up the church doors for Noon Prayer. Lorenzo needed help, and he needed it now. He had been out of work for too many months, and Conya was close to kicking him out of the house if he didn't bring home some money. She didn't even care what kind of work he got, just so he started bringing home the dough! He had been tempted to go out and start dealing. He knew from high school experience how easy it was to buy a little, turn it over, buy a little more, divide it out, cut it, and pretty soon he could be making a nice living. But he did not want to do that just for money! He wanted to live an honest life, working at an honest job, bringing home honest money.

She had threatened to keep Ebony from him if he didn't come through, but he had to do it the right way, the legal way. He kept praying, and he knew God would open a window for him. His grandmother had often said that God doesn't close a door without opening a window, and he wanted so desperately to believe that, but, so far, it was not happening.

A couple of guys walked by the church, not even noticing he was there on the porch, and he could tell they were high on something. They were swaying, laughing, fumbling around with something in their fingers. No, he would not allow himself to be responsible for anyone acting like that. He wanted to be able to help people, not cause them harm.

He smiled in spite of himself. He was thinking like a

doctor: 'I will do no harm.' He could never be a doctor, because there was no way he could get through all that schooling, but he could help people in other ways. Maybe he could be a pastor. His pastor was always helping people.

The church door opened and Pastor Stronghart didn't seem a bit surprised to see Lorenzo waiting for him on the porch.

"Good morning, Brother Lorenzo!" Pastor Stronghart greeted him joyfully.

"Good morning, Pastor Stronghart," he replied, although not quite as joyfully. As he reached out to shake his hand, Pastor Stronghart pulled him into a hug.

"It is a beautiful day that the Lord has made," Pastor Stronghart said, as he propped open the front doors to the church.

"Yes, it is, Pastor," Lorenzo agreed, looking at the sky. He had not noticed how blue it was until just now. This was a rare day with no clouds in the sky.

Pastor Stronghart joined Lorenzo on the porch. "You are here early for Noon Prayer meeting," he remarked.

"I was hoping to have a chance to talk to you before prayer time, Pastor," Lorenzo said, leaning against one of the pillars.

"Do you want to come into my office?" Pastor Stronghart asked, "or can we talk right here?"

Lorenzo looked around and didn't see anyone else coming this way. "We can talk here, I guess."

"Okay," Pastor Stronghart said, standing near the

porch railing. "What is on your mind, my brother?"

"You know I lost my job a while back," Lorenzo began.

"Yes, that was about the time you started coming here," Pastor Stronghart reminded him.

"Yeah, that was why I started coming," Lorenzo said, "so all the church could pray for me that I would get another job. Well, I have been looking for work every week, and I have not even had one interview. I can't find anything in my field. I can't find any kind of work that I am qualified to do."

"Wait a minute, let's back up," Pastor Stronghart said, rolling his fingers in a backward motion, as if to rewind something. "You started coming to the church, and you have been coming every Sunday, so God will give you another job?"

"That's right," Lorenzo said, nodding his head. "My grandmother down in Louisiana taught me to always come to the Lord when I was in trouble."

"Brother Lorenzo, why do you have to wait until you are in trouble before you come to the Lord?" Pastor Stronghart asked.

"When I had a job, everything was going good for me, and with Conya and Ebony, so I didn't need to come to church," Lorenzo answered, shrugging his shoulders.

"Do you ever think that maybe God took away your job so you could look to Him for your blessings, instead of thinking you were doing it all yourself?" Pastor Stronghart asked.

"But I was the one working, and I was working hard, and I got that job all by myself," Lorenzo protested.

"But who gave you that job?" Pastor Stronghart asked.

"I got it myself," Lorenzo repeated, scratching his head.

"Let me put it this way: who blessed you with that job?" Pastor Stronghart asked.

"When you put it that way, God was the one who blessed me with the job," Lorenzo said. He looked up at the sky. "You are saying that God gave it to me, right?"

"That's right," Pastor Stronghart said, gazing out toward the street. "How long did you work there, at that job?"

"Four years, and I never missed a day of work," Lorenzo said.

"You worked there four years, and how many times did you thank Him for that job?" Pastor Stronghart asked, looking Lorenzo in the eye.

Lorenzo looked down and didn't answer his question.

"I didn't hear you, Brother Lorenzo," Pastor Stronghart said quietly.

"I didn't thank Him for it," he said, his voice just above a whisper. He kept his head hanging down.

"Brother Lorenzo, look at me," Pastor Stronghart said gently.

Lorenzo slowly lifted his head and met his pastor's eyes.

"Don't you think it's about time that you thanked Him for it?" Pastor Stronghart asked, nodding his head.

"But He took it away from me!" Lorenzo argued,

clenching his fists.

"I think it's kind of funny," Pastor Stronghart said, "that when you got the job, you got it on your own, but when you lost your job, God took it away from you. What does that say about your idea of God? Do you think that God is some big mean guy who lives in the sky, just waiting to snatch good things away from us?"

"No, of course not," Lorenzo said, relaxing a little. "That would be ridiculous."

"Well, then, do you think He is an errand boy, like a waiter, just waiting for you to ask Him for something so He can give it to you?" Pastor Stronghart asked.

"No," Lorenzo answered, yet thinking, that was not far from his impression of Him. Wasn't He waiting up in heaven to answer prayers?

"Brother Lorenzo, God is holy, God is mighty, God is high and lifted up," Pastor Stronghart said passionately. "God knows all about you. He has every hair on your head numbered, and if you lose any of them, He knows how many you have left. He cares about the little sparrows, and He cares all about you."

Lorenzo started feeling emotional, exactly what he did not want to do right now, but it was just that everything his pastor was saying reminded him so much of what his grandmother would say. He looked down at his feet.

"I think you should start by thanking God for the job you did have before you start asking Him for another job," Pastor Stronghart suggested.

"I guess that is a good idea," Lorenzo agreed. He knew in his heart that his pastor was right.

"The next step," Pastor Stronghart said, getting down to business, "what kind of job do you want?"

"I just want a job, any job," Lorenzo said, turning his palms toward heaven, to catch the nearest falling job.

"Come on, my brother, be honest with God and with yourself," Pastor Stronghart said.

"I am," Lorenzo said.

"You would take a job baby-sitting?" Pastor Stronghart asked.

"I didn't mean that kind of job."

"What about mowing lawns?"

"Well I could do that, but I don't have the equipment for it," Lorenzo said, shaking his head.

"Let us be specific with God," Pastor Stronghart said. "What kind of job would you really like?"

"You mean, what would be my dream job?" Lorenzo asked, daring to dream.

"Yes, God has the best for you, so why don't you ask Him for it?" Pastor Stronghart said boldly.

"Yeah, why don't I ask Him for it?" Lorenzo said, gaining some courage. "He has the best for me, so why am I asking Him for anything less?"

"So, what would be your dream job?" Pastor Stronghart asked.

"Well, I love to drive, so I guess my dream job would be driving," Lorenzo said. He didn't even have a car, but he loved to drive.

"Do you have your CDL license?" Pastor Stronghart

asked.

"No, but I have my driver's license," Lorenzo answered.

"That is a good start. Why don't you get your CDL license?"

"I never really thought about doing that. I figured I would probably just keep working in some warehouse."

"Let's get you started on getting your CDL license, see what you have to do, if you have to take a class to be able to take the test."

"Pastor Stronghart, that is the best idea I have heard in months." Lorenzo's attitude had done a complete turn-around, and he was now looking forward to his future.

"One more thing, Brother Lorenzo," Pastor Stronghart said. "Let's go inside and pray and thank the Lord before you do anything."

"Pastor, I think that is actually the best idea I have heard in years," Lorenzo said, slapping Pastor Stronghart on his back and following him into the church building.

## Pastor Fields

On Sunday morning, Pastor Fuente Fields and his wife, Tammy, were riding the city bus, on their way to church. He watched out the window as the houses and neighborhoods passed by, reminding him of how quickly his life was passing by. At age seventy-four, he was at least twenty years older than Pastor Stronghart, and he could not figure how so many years had gone by so quickly.

He thought about the time when he decided to go into the ministry and he could not find anyone to sponsor him, or to even encourage him. After he had spent ten years in the navy, he had worked hard as a clerk in the finest men's store downtown for fourteen years – then the downtown went downhill, and the store closed. He was never able to find another job after that, but he felt his calling to go into the ministry, to serve others. Tammy had been hoping he would find another job to supplement her disability check, but she was proud of him when he said he wanted to be a minister and help other people. She gladly would have worked to help with the finances, but no one would hire a woman who had no work experience and had ten to twenty seizures per week. When Fuente told her he was quitting his job search to start studying to be a minister, she was secretly happy that he would be home with her, to take care of her and watch over her. He was so patient with her, so she knew he would make a good minister.

He had been a minister for more than ten years, thanks to Pastor Stronghart. Other pastors in the area had told Fuente that they didn't have room on their staff for another minister, but Pastor Stronghart had welcomed him with open arms. He had given him his chance, he had ordained him, and he eventually had made him an associate pastor at Total Missionary Baptist Church.

Pastor Fields looked at Tammy as she stared straight ahead. Was she having a seizure? Most people thought of a seizure as causing a person to lie on the ground while the muscles jerked, but Tammy often had seizures that made her stare straight ahead. Sometimes they lasted just a few seconds, other times they lasted minutes. She could never be left alone, and he was thankful for Joanne, their nosy, older neighbor lady, who was always willing to come over and stay with her when he had to go somewhere.

Tammy turned her head and looked at him. She gave him a loving smile. If she had just had a seizure, it had been a quick one and was over now.

"Can we go to Burger Ranch after church and get a milkshake and some French fries?" she asked, as innocently as a child would be asking. "They give you so many fries, and they are so long, and the milkshakes are made from real ice cream and they are so thick and smooth."

"We will have to see," Fuente told her. He was hoping Pastor Stronghart would have him preach for a few minutes and then take up an offering for him. He didn't have any money, not even for the offering. The thought flashed through his mind that if he didn't spend any money on cigarettes, they might have a little more spending money, but he quickly dismissed that thought. He was only buying one or two packs a week now, maybe three. He was down from two packs a day, and he was asking the Lord to help him quit completely.

"I hope we do," Tammy said, settling back into her seat.

"Oh, here is where we get off," Fuente said, pulling the cord to request a stop.

They got off the bus and began to walk to the church. The bus stop was about seven blocks from the church, but Fuente and his wife were accustomed to walking all over town. Today, at least it hadn't started raining yet. The day was overcast but not cold.

As they were crossing the street, two older ladies were approaching them from the other side of the street. Suddenly, Fuente was overcome with pain, in his chest, his back, his arms, and he fell to the ground, right in the middle of the crosswalk. He did not lose consciousness, but he was in great pain for just a few seconds, then it began to subside.

"Are you okay?" one lady asked.

"Are you all right?" the other lady asked, as they both hovered over him.

"Quick, call 9-1-1," the first lady said.

"Do you have your cell phone?" the other lady asked.

"Oh, no, I left it in my coat pocket, back at your house," the first lady said.

"My husband!" Tammy shouted, leaning over him.

"I'm all right," Fuente said, as he began to regain his strength.

"I can go ask the neighbor if I can use her phone and call you an ambulance," one lady said.

"No, I am okay," Fuente insisted. "I just have to get to

the church and I will be fine." He took a deep breath. He had that goal in mind, knowing that everything would be all right if he could make it to the church.

"Where is your church?" one lady asked.

"It's just about two blocks ahead," he struggled to say.

"It's right up there," Tammy said, pointing to Total Missionary Baptist Church.

"Let us help you," the other lady insisted.

"My husband, Pastor Fuente Fields, is one of the ministers at the church," Tammy announced.

The ladies helped him get to his feet, steadying him as he stood. His pain was now gone.

"I can make it now," he said. "Thank you ladies both, thank you so much."

"We can walk you to the church," one lady offered, "to make sure you can make it there."

"Oh, no, thank you, though," he said, thanking them again.

"No, we insist," the other lady said, as they both nodded.

With Tammy on his right side, one lady on his left side and the other lady walking close behind him, they made it to the church in few minutes, walking slowly and deliberately.

Pastor Stronghart was standing at the door as they walked up the front steps.

"Good morning, Pastor, good morning, Sister Tammy," Pastor Stronghart said, with a big, welcoming smile on his face. He reached out to give hugs to Fuente and his wife. "Who is this you have with you?"

"Are you the pastor of this church?" one lady asked, before Pastor Fields could answer his question.

"Yes, I am Pastor Stronghart," he said, shaking her hand.

"This man fell in the street, right in the crosswalk, just a couple of blocks away, and we wanted to call 9-1-1, but he said he would be okay if he could just make it to the church," she said.

"Are you okay, Pastor?" Pastor Stronghart asked, concern filling his face.

"Yeah, I just, um, I guess I just tripped," he said, not wanting to make anything of the incident.

"I really think this man should go to the hospital," one of the ladies said, shaking her finger at him, as if he were a disobedient child. "At your age, if you are falling in the street, you need to be checked out."

"Pastor Stronghart, all I really need is prayer," Pastor Fields said.

"Are you sure?" Pastor Stronghart asked, examining him closely.

"All he really needs is prayer," Tammy repeated.

Pastor Fields silently thanked her for her support. All he needed was prayer, and then he would be fine.

"Well, then, let us pray right now," Pastor Stronghart said, putting his hand on Pastor Fields' shoulder. "Father, in the precious name of Jesus, we ask that You touch this pastor right now, with Your healing virtue, from the top of his head to the bottom of his feet.  Touch, heal, revive, renew, right now, in the name of Jesus.  We give You all the honor, all the glory and all the praise right now.  In Jesus' name we pray.  Amen."

"Now I know I am fine," Pastor Fields said, as he guided his wife into the church building.

"You ladies are welcome to join us this morning, for our morning worship service," Pastor Stronghart said. "We are going to be starting in about fifteen minutes."

"Thank you, and it was nice meeting you, but we really have to go now," one of the ladies said.

Pastor Fields looked back to see the ladies running down the steps of the church, acting as if they had seen a ghost.

"We'll see you later!" Pastor Stronghart called to the ladies.  He watched them as they ran away from the church.

"Bye-bye!" Tammy shouted after them.

"They will be back," Pastor Stronghart said confidently, "when God calls them back, in His timing."

## Patricia

Flopping from one house to another for just a few nights at a time with three kids was not working out for Patricia. She was sick of getting high and she was tired of moving her babies from one place to another. They couldn't stay clean, and they couldn't keep anything, not even a change of clothes. They needed a home. It was time to put their needs before hers. She had to grow up and be a good mother.

She thought about the last time they had been really happy, really comfortable, and that was when they had happened upon the church that Kandy had called a lighthouse a few months ago. That pastor was really nice. So was that other young man who was there. Today was Sunday. She could take the kids to church, and maybe they could get some help.

"Come on, let's get ready to go," she said, rousing them from their borrowed blankets on the floor.

"Where?" Lonny asked.

"Come on, get up," she said, irritated. They never moved fast enough for her. She always had to push them, pull them, get them moving.

They would have to wear what they had on, since these were their best clothes. No one would know they had been wearing them for the last week, or had it been two weeks? Anyway, no one she knew ever went to church, so no one at church would know what they had been wearing.

"Come on, let's go," she said angrily, sweeping all the

blankets with her foot into a pile in the corner.

"Mommy, I'm hungry," Kandy whined. "Can we eat now? You said we can eat in the morning. Is it morning now?"

"We will get something to eat later," Patricia said, trying to smooth Lesly's hair into place. Where would a person keep a comb in this house? Well, it didn't matter, her hair looked fine, for a baby.

She was finally able to coax them out of the house, relieved to see that it was not raining. They were only about ten blocks from the church. They would be able to make it there in no time.

"Mommy, where we going?" Kandy asked, dragging her feet.

"We are going back to the lighthouse," Patricia said, hoping to motivate her daughter into walking faster.

"The lighthouse?" Kandy asked excitedly. She began jumping up and down and she bounced in the direction they were walking. "Can we have a hot dog?"

"Hot dog!" Lonny shouted. He started bouncing beside Kandy.

"I don't know if they have hot dogs today," Patricia said, "but they will have something for us, I promise you."

## Carolina

For once, Carolina was ready to go to church on time. She was proud of herself and her new Bible studies system. Putting the lessons in the refrigerator was working, in two ways: she was studying the Bible regularly and she was eating less. She wanted to testify at church that she was eating more spiritual food and less physical food. She was excited that she was able to fit into a smaller pair of pants today, and she had not even been feeling hungry! She had more energy and her mind was more focused.

It was amazing how studying the Word of God had transformed her entire life! Now she understood what Sister Evelyn had been talking about. Wasn't it interesting, though, that the Bible studies were in one way what Evelyn needed, and in another way what Carolina needed? She had yet to figure that one out, but she didn't care. It was working, and she was having success!

Now that she had discovered a system that worked for her, she wanted to share it with everyone. Why hadn't anyone told her about this before? Why had she had to figure it out herself? Why had God put her through so many tests before she arrived at where she needed to be?

Her logical mind told her before she wanted to accept the reason: it was because if it had happened any other way, she would not have believed it. She had to go through all the struggles, all the failures, so she would know for herself that this was the one thing that worked for her. If anyone else had told her about this, she would not have believed him. After all, she was from Missouri, the 'Show Me' state, and she had to see it to believe it.

She knew from her Bible studies lesson that faith was believing even when you couldn't see it, and she was getting to that point, but right now, God had proved that His system worked for her.

Oh, that was hitting the nail on the head. It was not her system. It was God's system. All the time that she had tried to follow her own system, she had failed. She had to remember to give Him the glory, because He was leading her and she was merely following Him. She needed to remember that when she got to church so she could testify about it.

Finally, she had something to say, a great testimony! Oh, sure, she had spoken in church before, mostly when the attendance was very low, but just saying that God had saved her and God was keeping her and He was giving her joy wasn't very exciting for the others to hear. Now she had something important to say, a great thing God was doing in her life! Plus, people could look at her and see a change, a physical change, a decrease in her size! She was really excited about this.

Carolina got her Bible and went out to the car. She was so thrilled, she didn't acknowledge any part of the drive to church – suddenly, she was there! She parked in one of the spaces marked for the handicapped and thought, maybe soon she would not need to park in this space. After she lost more weight, she would be able to walk better. She would gladly give up a parking space nearest the church for the ability to walk a farther distance. She was already walking a bit better, and her back and knees and her feet were hurting a little bit less than they usually did.

As she entered the church, she saw that the crowd was

larger than the usual Sunday group. She was still early, but, for some reason, so were a lot of other people. Most of the regulars were there: the Stronghart family, Brother Jason and two of his friends, Pastor Fields and his wife, Brother Chester and Sister Sandra, Mother Judith, Brother Lorenzo and his girlfriend and their little girl, plus about ten people Carolina had never seen before. Today, in front of a large crowd, she was going to have the chance to really testify about her new Bible studies system – no, about God's Bible study system – the one that He had shown her, the one that was working for her.

Several people greeted her with a hug as she made her way to her usual seat on one side of the sanctuary. One day soon, she would not have to sit in this seat, because she would be able to easily fit in the pews. She smiled at the thought.

"Sister Carolina, you are looking very glorious today," Pastor Stronghart said, as he gave her a hug. "You seem to be glowing. I can see the glory of the Lord all over you today. You must be overflowing with the Spirit of God."

"Thank you," she said, suddenly humbled. She did not want to stand up and brag about what God had been doing for her. This was her private victory and she did not really want to tell everyone about it. Didn't Pastor Stronghart say, just about every week, that testimony service was not to glorify ourselves, but to glorify God? Yes, her testimony could glorify God, but not if she presented it proudly.

The service started and Carolina had a hard time listening. Her mind was so distracted as she wondered if she should testify or not, and if she did, what should she say, and how should she say it. She halfway paid attention to the devotional service, the call to worship and the opening prayer because she knew testimonies would come next.

"Hasn't God been good?" Pastor Stronghart asked from the pulpit.

"All the time!" the congregation shouted, their standard response.

"Why is it, we only come to Him, we only want to talk to Him when we need something from Him?" Pastor Stronghart asked. "God wants to hear from us when things are good, as well as when things are bad, in times of joy as well as in times of trouble.

"Whatever you do, you should do it with enthusiasm. You should do everything to the glory of God. Come on, church! Glorify Him!" He raised his hands in the air.

A smattering of clapping and a few "Hallelujahs" were given in response.

"I get so tired of seeing Christians – I'm not talking about unsaved people, because they don't have anything to get happy about, they don't have any joy, I am talking about Christians –" Pastor Stronghart said, "walking around with their heads hanging down, and when you see them, they look like they have the entire world on their shoulders. What kind of testimony to the world is that? The world sees us and thinks that our problems are worse than theirs, because at least they get temporary relief in the bottle or at the bar or at the clubs.

"Brothers and sisters, we have the joy of Christ! And Jesus said, 'the joy I give you, no man can take away,' so let us show that joy to the world! I am not talking about Christmas here, I am talking about every day joy that Jesus gives us! The Bible tells us in Nehemiah 8:10 that the joy of the Lord is our strength! Do you feel defeated today? Do you feel like you are carrying the weight of the world? Turn it over to Jesus, and let Him work it out, because He can! He can! He can, today, work it out for you," he pointed toward the congregation, "and you, and you, right now!"

People began standing on their feet and cheering.

"He told us to bring our burdens to Him. He said to come to Him, all you who are heavy laden and He will give you rest! Do you need some rest today? Now, He was not talking about sitting back and resting! He was talking about giving us rest from the burden of sin!

"Oh, you don't hear me today! We are all here, we are all healthy, we have voices to praise Him, so, let us praise Him! Praise Him!" He began jumping up and down. "I could go to any hospital or nursing home or jail cell, or even to a funeral home and find someone who would give anything to be here today! And here we are, today, with our health and strength, and we can't even praise Him?

"Has He not done something great for you? Has He not given His life for you, so you can be at peace with God, and go to heaven? Oh, yes, He has! If nobody else wants to praise Him, I will praise Him, until the day I die! I will thank Him for all He is doing!"

The congregation was getting excited now, with the mothers of the church chanting, "Praise Him!" and "He's a wonder!" and the younger generation jumping up and down by their seats. People were raising their hands in praise, and a few were crying out to God.

"Hallelujah! Hallelujah! Hallelujah!" Pastor Stronghart shouted, as the praise began to subside. Sweat was streaming down his face. He wiped it with a handkerchief as he began to calm down a little. The rest of the congregation took their seats.

"Does anyone have a fiery testimony? I mean, a testimony that will make the rest of us jump out of our seats of complacency and praise God?"

Carolina had to be the first to say something. She did have a fiery testimony, and God had done great things for her!

"I do!" she shouted, before she could second-guess herself.

"Go ahead, Sister Carolina," Pastor Stronghart said. "Tell us why you have that heavenly glow all over you today."

Suddenly a strong feeling came over her and she could not tell about all God had done for her. The words she had rehearsed and memorized were all gone and suddenly, without any control, she began to sob.

"God is good," was all she was able to say, then she began blubbering, aware that everyone was staring at her. She lost all words and her nurse's mind wondered if she were having a stroke. Why could she not think of what she had just been about to say?

"Praise God!" Pastor Stronghart said. "Don't try to hold it back, Sister Carolina. Just let it all out."

"I miss my daughter, Patty," she said, immediately upset with herself. She had not wanted to bring that up here. Patty was gone, out of her life. She had left and she was not going to come back. Carolina may as well not even have a daughter. Unlike Sister Evelyn's daughter, Patty had told her mother she would never, ever see her again.

She heard whispers of, "She has a daughter?" and "I never knew she had a daughter." This was her family now. She could tell them and they would not make fun of her when she cried.

"Sister Carolina," Sister Judith said slowly, in her Southern drawl, "earth has no sorrow that heaven and Jesus cannot heal."

"My daughter, Patty…" Carolina began, as the church fell silent, hanging on her every word. Carolina was not sure what to say next. She got all choked up and Sister Stronghart came over to sit beside her and put her arm around her. This made things worse, because this woman who, until recently, was a stranger to her, was part of this new family, and her own daughter was not around any more.

"Let's all pray for Sister Carolina," Pastor Stronghart said, when he realized she couldn't continue, "and for her daughter, Patty. We don't have to wait to pray until prayer time, we can pray for them right now.

"Father, in the name of Jesus, we ask that You touch this mother, right here, right now, and comfort her. We ask that You touch her daughter, Patty, right now, where ever she is, whatever she is doing, and give her comfort as well. Father, we know You have heard us before, and we know You are hearing us right now, and we thank You in advance for what You are going to do. In the mighty name of Jesus we pray. Amen.

"Sister Carolina, it's already done! Let us thank Him for it! Thank You, Jesus! Thank You, Father! Thank You, Lord!"

"Thank You, Father," she was able to say, and she did feel a comfort, a touch from the Lord, a type of warmth moving through her entire body. She could never be able to describe it, but she could feel it, and it put a smile on her face.

All of a sudden the doors of the church burst open. Carolina could not believe her eyes. She blinked twice to be sure she wasn't hallucinating.

"Good morning, young lady," Pastor Stronghart said, turning toward the door as he was approaching the pulpit. "Find a seat, right over there will be fine. Brother Jason, can you help her with her children?"

Carolina stood up without even using her cane and looked directly at Pastor Stronghart.

"God sure does answer prayers, and He does not waste any time," she announced, loudly and boldly. "This is my daughter, Patty."

## Pastor Stronghart

Pastor Stronghart reflected on today's service and the miracles that had taken place. Sister Evelyn was now filled with joy and had volunteered to join the Food Bank Ministry. Brother Lorenzo had taken his CDL test and passed, opening the doors to many job possibilities. And Sister Carolina's daughter had appeared, as a direct answer to their prayer, along with the joy Sister Carolina now had, even before Sister Patricia had come into the building. How wonderful to see her family reunite, and for Sister Carolina to have a chance to meet two grandchildren she didn't even know she had until today.

Also, after much prayer about the situation, Pastor Stronghart had asked Sister Carolina if she would consider the position of church treasurer, and she willingly agreed. She had really had a day. She had come into the building with a new joy, having been filled with the Holy Spirit, her prayer to see her daughter had been answered, and she had become the church treasurer. Yes, today was truly a day when many of God's plans came to realization, and Pastor Stronghart was thanking and praising Him within his heart.

## Shannon

The doorbell rang and Shannon skittered down the steps to answer it.

"Brother Chester!" she said, happy to see him. "Come in, come in. What brings you here this evening? Is everything okay?"

"Good evening, Mrs. Stronghart," he said, removing his cap as he entered the house. "Is the pastor at home?"

"No, he is still out," she said, opening her palm to the home, "but come on in and have something to drink. Do you want some pop or water or juice or something? He should be back in a little while. He went over to the hospital to visit a family that was just in a car accident."

"Oh, glory be," Brother Chester said, coming into the kitchen. "Yes, a pop would be fine, any kind, whatever you have, just so it is not diet."

She got a glass from the cupboard. "Do you want ice in your glass?"

"No, please don't go to any trouble," he said. "I just want to ask Pastor a question. I just took my wife to her sister's house, and I told her I had an errand to run. I need to go back and get her in a few minutes."

"Is it anything I can help you with?" she asked, handing him a glass and a can of pop.

"Thank you. Well…" he began, dragging out the word, then pouring the soda into the glass, "it's for my wife."

"For Sister Sandra?" she asked. "What do you mean?"

"As you know, our thirty-fifth wedding anniversary is coming up in a couple of weeks," he said, "and it lands on a Sunday."

"Which is also Sister Sandra's birthday," Shannon added.

"Yes, and so this is why I want to do something special for her and surprise her," he said, beginning to get emotional. "I love her so much, and I want her to know it."

"We all know how much you love her," she said, thinking that they were truly two people who had been made for each other. They had a language of their own, a body language, a gesturing language, a language of just looking lovingly at each other and knowing the other so well. She wondered how Brother Chester would ever be able to keep a secret from his wife, since it seemed like they could just about read each other's minds.

"I don't know how to show her," Brother Chester said, breaking down.

"Brother Chester, you show her every day how much you love her," Shannon said. Their love for each other was so obvious; Shannon hoped she and her husband still had that kind of love for each other after thirty-five years of marriage. They had a good start, but the Deacons were a great example to follow.

"But I really want to do something so special for her, something that she will never forget until the day the Lord takes her home," Brother Chester said. "I just can't think of anything. And since it is on a Sunday, I don't want to take her out of town. I want to go to church, like we do every Sunday, and then somehow surprise her. Do you have any ideas?"

She was saved by the sound of the garage door opening.

"There's the pastor," she said, hurrying off to meet him. She hoped he had a great suggestion for Brother Chester; and, knowing her husband, he would.

"Hello, my Dear," he said, greeting her with a kiss. "Is that Brother Chester's car in the drive?"

"Yes, he is upstairs in the kitchen," she said. "How is the family? Is everyone okay?"

"The father has a broken leg and the Mom has a possible neck injury, but the two children are fine," he said, removing his overcoat and hanging it in the coat closet. "They really need prayer. They were so happy to see me."

"Oh, thank God," Shannon said.

"So, what does Brother Chester need?" he asked, as they headed up the stairs.

"He needs some ideas from you," she said.

"Good evening, Brother Chester!" the pastor said, giving him a hug.

"Good evening, Pastor," Chester replied, visibly relieved to be able to talk to him.

"Did you get something to drink?"

"Yes, your wife gave me a can of pop," he said, holding up his glass as proof.

"What brings you to our neck of the woods this evening? How is your wife? Is everything okay?"

"Yes, yes, she is fine," Brother Chester said, taking a sip of his pop. "I took her over to see her sister. I need to pick her up in a few minutes."

"Praise the Lord," the pastor said.

"I was just telling your wife, Mrs. Stronghart, that our thirty-fifth wedding anniversary is coming up in a couple of weeks."

"That's right! Congratulations!" He filled a glass with water and sat down at the table with Brother Chester.

"I want to do something really special for my wife," Brother Chester said. "Her birthday and our anniversary are going to be on a Sunday, so I don't want to take her out of town, but I just don't know what to do to make it an anniversary to remember."

"Brother Chester, whatever you do in love, she will remember. It is not about getting the biggest gift or the best gift or the most expensive gift, but whatever you give her, give from your heart."

"But what can I give her?" he asked, shaking his head. "What is that special something? She doesn't need anything, and she has a whole room full of stuffed animals."

"And each one of those stuffed animals was a gift of love," the pastor reminded him.

"I was thinking about maybe giving her an anniversary ring, but is that really special enough?"

"Brother Chester, you know what would make it very special?" the pastor asked enthusiastically.

"What's that?"

"Why don't you renew your wedding vows after church on that Sunday?"

"Renew our wedding vows?" Brother Chester looked puzzled.

"We can have a renewal ceremony, to renew your wedding vows," he said.

"Brother Chester, maybe you can get her a new dress for that Sunday, and she will think that is her anniversary present, then, after church service, we will have a wedding ceremony, and you can give her the anniversary ring!" Shannon said, getting excited about the whole idea.

"I think she would love that," Brother Chester said, nodding his head and smiling.

"We can get the whole church involved," the pastor said. "Dr. Martin can play the organ, the kids can be flower girl and ring bearer, and we can get a nice certificate and have it framed."

"And we can make a wedding cake and take pictures, just like your first wedding," Shannon said.

"Oh, this will be better than our first wedding," Brother Chester said. "She never had the wedding she really wanted, because we eloped on her eighteenth birthday."

"You eloped?" Shannon asked. "You never told us that."

"Sandra didn't want me to tell anyone about it," Brother Chester said. "You know, this is going to be the best gift ever. She is going to get her fancy wedding, like she always wanted! But – shhhh! We have to keep it a secret."

"Oh, we will keep it a secret," the pastor said. "You just get the ring and the dress and have her at church on that Sunday, and we will take care of all of the details."

"Wedding details, we've got them covered," Shannon said, tapping her head, as she was already beginning to make a list of what needed to be done.

## Officer Shotgun

As he surfed through the channels on cable, Ted Shotgun could not believe his eyes. That drug-dealing pastor was on television! That was the proof, right there, that he was into shady dealings! How could he have his own television program? Television programming time was very expensive, and yet, there he was, acting like he was preaching or something. The information on the channel guide said this was a one-hour program, so that must cost him a pretty penny. Everything was adding up: he had an expensive car, he had a television program, he did his dealings in a known drug-infested neighborhood. The only thing was, he was sneaky.

Ted kept on the program with the sound muted, watched the so-called pastor moving around, pointing at the camera, appearing to be reading from some book. At first, he didn't want to turn up the sound, because he knew everything the man was saying was just nonsense. As he watched him, he was getting more and more angry. Finally, he had to know what he was saying, how he was tricking people into sending him money, because that was what TV preachers did. He turned up the sound.

After a few sentences, he was surprised that the man had not yet asked for money or donations. He was just talking about church stuff, the Bible, or something, but then he seemed to be speaking in some kind of code. He wasn't making any sense. He was speaking gibberish, baloney.

Then it started to make sense: he was using some kind of underground drug code to get to his listeners. Only those in that drug sub-culture would know what he was talking about. Although at the police station they regularly had trainings about the latest fads in the underworld, this was something he had not heard before. Perhaps because this man had a Southern accent, he probably had connections to the Afro-American drug sub-culture from other parts of the country. What else could he mean when he said, 'fill my cup, Lord,' and 'be drunk with the Spirit?' Yes, he would have to decode this druggie language, and when he had enough evidence, he would present it to his captain, and they would make the bust, plain and simple.

He just had to figure it out first, and he would. He would not quit until he had shut down this whole operation.

## Pastor Stronghart

The couple stood before Pastor Stronghart in his office. He had never seen them before, but they were acting like they knew him. The man had called him earlier and asked if they could stop by and talk to him, but he would not give him a hint why they wanted to see him.

"My wife and I are here –" the man began, clearly tense.

"I am Pastor Stronghart," he interrupted. He liked to do things decently and in order, not just jump into the situation without any introduction. "I don't believe we have met before; or have we?"

"No, we have not," the man said. "My name is Roger Dotbitty, and this is my wife, Regina Dotbitty." He put his arm tightly around her shoulders, seemingly causing her discomfort.

"Brother Roger, Sister Regina, it is so nice to meet you," Pastor Stronghart said. "Are you from around here?"

"We moved up here from California a couple years ago," Roger said.

"Have a seat," Pastor Stronghart asked, motioning to the little couch behind them.

They sat obediently, without looking at each other.

"Good afternoon, and before we get started, let us have a word of prayer," Pastor Stronghart said.

"Father, in the name of Jesus, I ask that You come in here with us today. Touch this couple, whatever their situation may be, and help me, as I give advice that comes only from You. Not my will, but Thy will be done. Give me Your wisdom, that is so much higher than my wisdom, that I may be a blessing and glorify You. In the name of Jesus we ask these things. Amen.

"What part of California are you from?" Pastor Stronghart asked. Knowing a little about their background would help him know more about them, and that was his specialty. He was a people person. He knew many, many people, and even if he didn't remember all the names, he remembered all the details about their circumstances: when and where they had met; if their parents were still living, and if so, where, and if not, when and where they had passed away; if family members were in the hospital or in jail, or sick or in distress; if they had children, and if so, how many children, their ages, and where they were.

"We lived in Santa Barbara for awhile, about three years, but before that, we lived in Arizona for two years," Roger said.

Pastor Stronghart noticed that the wife had not said a word. She had an invisible wall around her, giving the impression that she did not want to be there. He didn't take it personally – it was more likely something about her husband that was bothering her.

"Did you move here, or are you just visiting?" Pastor Stronghart asked.

"We live in Portland," Roger said. "We moved here because of my job. I work for Nike."

"Oh, do you work over on MLK Boulevard?" Pastor Stronghart asked.

"Yeah, that's where I am most of the time," Roger said.

He seemed to be getting irritated that he was not directing the conversation.

"So, what brings you here?" Pastor Stronghart asked, ready to get down to business, or at least, find out the reason they wanted to see him.

"I told you, we moved here because of my job!" Roger shouted, leaning forward on the couch, looking like he was about to pounce on Pastor Stronghart's desk. "Are you not paying attention?"

Pastor Stronghart did not let Roger's erratic behavior upset him. He smiled at the couple, who were staring angrily at him. "I am asking, what brings you here, to my office?"

"Oh, yes, of course," Roger said, settling back on the couch a little. "We saw you on TV last week."

"Oh, you saw it in Portland?" Pastor Stronghart asked. He was surprised, since he didn't know the TV Ministry was playing in Portland, but this was good news to him. He wanted to get the Word of God out everywhere, in every way he could. A helpful local sponsor must have picked it up on the community access channel. "That is wonderful!"

"That is the reason we are here," Roger said, as if that explained it all.

"I see," said Pastor Stronghart, nodding, although he did not see what point Roger was trying to make.

"You said something on TV, and we wanted to come and check it out," Roger said, still not revealing their true intent for being there.

"Do you remember which program you saw?" Pastor

Stronghart asked, looking from Roger to his wife. "The title of the sermon, perhaps?"

"What? No, of course not!" Roger shouted, as his wife turned her head away from him, to look out the window. "That is not why we are here, to talk about the sermon! It was the one that was on last week!"

Pastor Stronghart put up his hands in defense. "Brother Roger, there is no need to shout," he said calmly.

"You said something, and I want to talk to you about it," Roger said, gritting his teeth. He looked at his wife's indifference and then snapped his head back to look at Pastor Stronghart.

Pastor Stronghart waited for him to continue.

"She is my wife!" Roger yelled, slamming his hand down on the arm of the couch.

"Yes, that is what you said when you introduced her," Pastor Stronghart said, nodding.

"She is so cold, and she ignores me," Roger said. "You said on TV, and we both heard you, that a wife should respond to her husband, and she is not responding! She just – she just lays there!"

"Do you love her?" Pastor Stronghart asked.

"She is my WIFE!" Roger demanded.

"Do you love her?" Pastor Stronghart asked again.

"We have been married for seven years!" Roger shouted.

"Do you love her?" Pastor Stronghart asked quietly.

"Why do you keep asking me that question?" Roger asked, visibly frustrated.

"Do you love me?" Regina asked, her voice just above a whisper. She was looking into her hands, not looking at her husband.

"You don't treat me right!" he yelled, causing her to flinch.

"Do you ever tell her that you love her?" Pastor Stronghart asked.

"Why should I have to do that? She's *my wife*. She knows me and she knows how I feel about her."

"You got that right," Regina mumbled, again looking out the window.

"See?" Roger asked triumphantly. "I do NOT need to tell her every day how I feel about her. She already knows."

"Let me ask you this," Pastor Stronghart said. "Are you Christians? Because my message about marriage was for Christians. People who are not believers in Christ have different standards for marriage."

"Of course we are Christians!" Roger shouted. "What else would we be? Mouseketeers? Do you think, just because we lived in California, we are not Christians? Oh, don't put us in a category like that!"

"Do you attend a church?" Pastor Stronghart asked gently, not letting Roger's elevated mood have an effect on him.

"A person does NOT have to attend a church to be a Christian!" Roger shouted.

"I agree with you, but I am asking if you have a church home."

"We don't believe in all that," Roger said. "We are just good people, we believe in God and we live good lives."

"The Bible tells us to not forsake the assembling of ourselves with other believers in Christ," Pastor Stronghart said.

"I don't care what the Bible says!" Roger shouted.

"Then I will not be able to help you," Pastor Stronghart said.

"Please," Regina said softly, pleading with her eyes, "help us."

"I really don't know what I can tell you," Pastor Stronghart said, "because you two do not believe the same things I believe. My teaching won't help you. When I counsel with couples, I make sure they are Christians before we start, because if they are not Christians, nothing I tell them can help them."

"What are you talking about?" Roger yelled. "I told you, we ARE Christians. What more do you want?"

"Do you believe Jesus is the Son of God?" Pastor Stronghart asked.

"Yeah, sure He is," Roger said. "He is a Son of God and I am a son of God and you are a son of God. Everyone is, because God is our Father. You should know that. You are a preacher."

"Do you believe Jesus died on the cross for your sins, and for my sins, and for the sins of the world, and that God raised Him from the dead on the third day, with all power in His hands? That He was raised by resurrection power, power over death?"

"What does that have to do with anything?" Roger asked. "Do you believe that Buddha died by overdosing on psychedelic mushrooms?"

"I don't know anything about that," Pastor Stronghart said, "but I do know for a fact that Jesus rose from the dead, and that He went back to glory, and He sent the Holy Spirit to lead us and guide us into all truth and righteousness."

"Well, isn't that the cat's pajamas?" Roger asked. "What on earth does that have to do with our marriage? Can you help us, or not?"

"I am not sure you really want my help," Pastor Stronghart stated.

"I believe," Regina said, looking up at Pastor Stronghart.

Her husband looked at her as if she were a talking giraffe. "You believe all that," he said, nodding his head in a demeaning manner.

"What I will tell you is this," Pastor Stronghart said. "The Bible says in Ephesians, husbands are to love their wives the same way Christ loves the church. Christ died for the church. Would you die for your wife?"

"What about the part that says wives are to submit to their husbands?" Roger asked smugly.

"The word 'submit' is actually an unfortunate translation," Pastor Stronghart explained. "In the original language, the word means 'respond.' A wife is to respond to her husband, which means that you show love to her, and she responds to your love with her love."

Roger sat back in his seat looking very uncomfortable.

Pastor Stronghart noticed a slight smile on Regina's face, the first emotion she had shown since they had arrived. They both looked at Pastor Stronghart expectantly, waiting for him to condemn one or the other.

"When a man comes to me and tells me that his wife is cold toward him, I immediately know how he has been treating her," Pastor Stronghart said. "Now, Brother Roger, gently take your wife's hands in your hands."

Roger hesitated, but he did as he was asked.

"Now, Brother Roger, do you love your wife?"

"Yes, I do," he said meekly.

"Why don't you tell her that you love her?"

"You mean, right now?" Roger swallowed forcefully.

"Yes, right now. Tell her that you love her," Pastor Stronghart instructed.

"Honey, I love you," Roger said mechanically, looking directly at Pastor Stronghart as he spoke.

"Okay, that is a start," Pastor Stronghart said. "Now, look at your wife, and, only if you do love her, tell her that you love her. And, Sister Regina, you look at your husband while he is speaking to you."

They behaved as if this were the hardest thing they had ever had to do. Their faces were like opposite magnets, not wanting to turn toward each other at the same time.

"Do we have to do this?" Roger asked, gulping.

"Do you want my help, or don't you?" Pastor Stronghart asked.

"Yes," they both whispered at the same time, as they

finally were able to look at each other.

Pastor Stronghart witnessed a transformation move through this couple as he prayed within. Roger's face softened, and Regina's indifference melted as they looked into each other's eyes. Roger took his right hand and touched Regina's hair. She gave him a sweet smile.

"Regina?" Roger said timidly.

"Yes, Roger?" she said.

"I love you so much," he said, as a tear began to make a trail from his eye.

"I love you, too, my husband," Regina responded. She touched his cheek with her fingertips.

Pastor Stronghart said softly, "The Bible says that the husband is to be the aggressor and the wife is to respond to her husband, so, Brother Roger, you treat her with love first, and she is to respond to you with love. Tell her you love her. Show her you love her. Be tender toward her. Speak well of her to others. After all, the man and woman have become one in marriage, so she is part of you, part of your own body. You would never treat your foot badly because it wasn't as pretty as your hand, would you?"

Roger laughed. "No, of course not. They have two different purposes, and I have to take care of them both."

"Exactly," Pastor Stronghart said, nodding, as he observed the couple who were acting as if they were newly in love. "You take care of yourself, but you also take care of your wife. And when you do that, you will find that she will also take care of you."

"So, you are saying it was all my fault?" Roger asked, still looking at his wife.

"A marriage is not a fifty-fifty relationship," Pastor Stronghart said. "It has to be that each one is giving one hundred percent to each other, and all to Jesus. Jesus is the foundation of a Christian marriage, and the husband and wife are the two pillars that stand upon Him, holding up each other. If you say you are giving fifty percent to your marriage, what are you giving the other fifty percent to? And what happens when one of you is sick, and you are not able to give even fifty percent? You have to each give all of yourself to the other, in order to make your marriage strong, and to make your relationship worthwhile."

"So, you are not saying it was all my fault?" Roger asked, stuck on that one point.

"I am not going to put the blame on either of you," Pastor Stronghart said, "but if you want your marriage to be strong, you need to consider the principles we have discussed today. Brother Roger, did you see how your wife responded to you when you changed your attitude toward her?"

"Oh, yeah, did I ever!" Roger exclaimed.

"And Sister Regina, did you feel a difference when your husband made that one small change?"

"Yes, Pastor," she said with a smile. "But will he stay like this? Will you, Honey?"

Roger looked to Pastor Stronghart for the answer.

"He will if he wants you to continue to respond in a positive manner to him," Pastor Stronghart said.

"Oh, yes, I do, so, oh, yes, I will!" Roger said, nodding.

Pastor Stronghart thought that Roger understood, but only time would tell. "I would like to invite you to come to our Sunday service," he said. "It starts at eleven o'clock on Sunday morning. Then you can meet my wife."

"Yeah, that was what brought us here in the first place," Roger said, suddenly recalling something. "The way you spoke about your wife, so loving, and you have been married, like, more than twenty years or something? That love you talked about, that was what made us decide to come and talk to you, because of the love you expressed about your wife during your sermon. I thought, 'if he can love his wife like that, I should be able to love my wife like that.' So we came here so you could teach us." He held his wife's hand.

"Just remember, this is not like a lesson that you can memorize and do," Pastor Stronghart said. "My love for my wife comes from Christ. He is the One who keeps refilling me and giving me more love for her, every day. You know, the more love I give her, the more love Jesus gives me to share with her."

"Huh!" Roger said, a light going on in his brain. "So, it is not just the way you act toward her, and she responds to you?"

"No, my actions come from my heart, and my heart is filled and refilled with the love of Christ." Pastor Stronghart said.

"How do you do that?" Regina asked, leaning slightly toward him.

"By studying His Word every day, I get a refilling of His Spirit," Pastor Stronghart said, "and also I pray. I talk to Him in prayer and He talks to me through His Word." He tapped on the cover of his Bible.

"You make it sound so simple," Roger said, throwing

his hands up in the air.

"God did not make it hard," Pastor Stronghart said, "but He does require diligence, persistence. He actually makes it quite easy."

"Well, Pastor, we just might have to take you up on that," Roger said, nodding his head slowly.

"Pastor, when I saw you on TV," Regina confessed, looking down at her hands, "I just prayed that some day my husband could love me the same way you love your wife. I think we can do it. Thank you." When she looked up at Pastor Stronghart, he could see her face was stained with tears, as she gave him a sincere smile.

"Yes, thank you, Pastor," Roger added.

"You can only do it with Jesus," Pastor Stronghart reminded them. "You can't do it on your own. No matter how hard you try, you will get weak. Your strength will eventually fail. You can only be successful with Jesus."

## Evelyn

What a wonderful day it was turning out to be! Evelyn looked at the sun peeking through the clouds for a sun break, and she was enjoying every second of it. She scurried through her house, dusting and straightening, as if she were getting ready for a visitor; but, no, she was keeping her home sparkling clean just for herself. She sang a bit of a tune that she remembered from Sunday service about thanking God for one more day, for one more chance to praise Him. She was so filled with joy!

She could not recall a time in her life – ever – when she had been so happy every day, and she attributed it all to her study of the Bible. God's Word was truly alive in her, as she learned more about Him and about His character every day, and grew closer to Him every day.

After she had been studying her Bible and doing the lessons for about three months, she had gone to Pastor Stronghart to ask him where he thought she should volunteer to minister. He gave her a list of places: the hospital, several nursing homes, the food bank and in a day care for under privileged children. He asked her to pray and ask the Lord where He wanted her to be, so she took the list home and read it over before and after her Bible studies time.

On the third day, when she returned to Pastor Stronghart to tell him which ministry she had chosen, she wanted to say she would volunteer in the hospital in the newborn ward, but the words that came out of her mouth were "food bank." She knew instantly that this was where God wanted her, even though she may have preferred to work with newborn babies. Now she was working with the meal delivery program, taking lunches to seniors three days per week, on the days she had off from work: Tuesdays, Wednesdays and Thursdays.

What a blessing that ministry was becoming! She had twenty-six people on her route, and many of them loved to talk to her about their faith. She was so happy she could be a joyful witness to them, bringing them cheer as well as meals. Some would ask her to pray with them, like Alice Fisher, who usually didn't see anyone else all week besides her, but she wanted to stay living in her own home. Mrs. Fisher had stopped driving long ago, and at age 97, she was as spry as a teenager. She was just lonely, and Evelyn was the only companion she had. They usually spent a good twenty minutes discussing Bible passages before Evelyn had to leave to continue her deliveries. When she first started delivering meals, Evelyn's route had taken her about ninety minutes to complete. Now, since she talked and ministered with all of her delivery clients, she usually spent more than three hours delivering the meals, and she loved every minute of it.

Her boss and her co-workers had noticed her new attitude, too. They often made remarks about how chipper she was, how her smile was lighting up the room like rays of sunshine, how nothing ever got her down anymore. She knew her life transformation had come about because she was studying the Word of God, and He was filling her with joy that kept on flowing from her, and peace that people couldn't understand. Of course, she still missed Marilyn, but now her life was full and active, instead of how it had been, empty and hopeless.

She glanced at the clock and grabbed her purse. She did not want to be late to meet Sister Stronghart. They had a wedding cake to make today!

## Sandra

The church service seemed to be passing so quickly, but Sandra was uncomfortable. She felt like she had eaten too much, either during her first breakfast at home, or her second breakfast at the Strongharts' home. She was also just a bit upset that nobody had mentioned her birthday or her wedding anniversary. She knew Chester had not forgotten: they had discussed it a few weeks ago, and he had never, ever since she was five years old, forgotten her birthday. She had snooped around at home while he was at work, looking for a gift, but she had not found even a clue that he had purchased anything: no receipt, no wrapping paper had been taken out of the closet, nothing new in the house or rearranged to hide something new. At this point, she just wanted the service to end so they could go home.

Well, he had bought her a new dress, which she was wearing for church, but he bought her new dresses a few times every year. He had selected a very beautiful blue dress, a rather fancy one, but he had not mentioned that it was an anniversary present, or even a birthday present. She leaned forward in her seat to try to relieve the pressure on her back. Since she had gained a little weight, her back had been bothering her more and more often.

She tried to concentrate on the sermon while Pastor Stronghart was preaching, but she kept thinking that something was wrong. Could Chester have forgotten about this special day? She glanced sideways at him, and he seemed to be enjoying himself, the same way he did every Sunday. The rest of the congregation was having a great time. They had overlooked her birthday, and they were just going on with the service, as if this were another regular day! She did not want to pout in church, but Chester was going to hear about it on the way home. She had thought that she would not mention anything unless he did, but now, she was getting hot under the collar. She would insist that he take her out to dinner – even though she wasn't really hungry right now. After service, he would take her to a fancy restaurant, whether they were hungry or not: she would make sure of it.

Pastor Stronghart was winding down his sermon and he was giving an invitation for anyone who wanted to accept Jesus to come forth. No one did. She was pretty sure that everyone in the building today had already accepted Him. Then Pastor Stronghart was asking if anyone wanted to join the church, if they didn't have a church home. No one came forward for that, either. Finally, he asked if anyone needed special prayer. That young girl, Patricia, the one with the three children, came forward and the church members prayed for them.

Sandra looked around her seat so she could collect her purse and her other belongings, to get ready to go.

"Sister Sandra," Pastor Stronghart said, startling her, "can you come up here, please?"

"Yes, Pastor," she said as she stood. She figured he probably wanted her to pray for someone, so she obediently went up in front of the congregation.

"Do you have your song book with you?" he asked, when she got up beside him.

"I left it in the car," she said, confused. She had an old hymnal that had been her grandmother's, and once in awhile a member would select a song to sing from it. "Do you need it for something?"

"Can you bring it inside for a minute?" Pastor Stronghart asked. "It has a song that I want to read out loud."

She was going to ask Chester to go and get it, but he was nowhere in sight. Good timing, he must have gone to the men's room right at that very moment.

"Sure, Pastor, I'll go get it," she said, getting her car keys out of her purse. "I will be right back."

She felt a little bit guilty since she had not been paying attention at the end of the service, and she was not quite sure why her pastor wanted her song book, but she went outside, across the street to the parking lot, and opened the car door. She didn't see the hymnal on the back seat, where she thought she had left it. She rummaged through the coats and blankets and papers and shoes – shoes? Why did they have shoes in the car? She would need to be more active in cleaning out the car. Starting tomorrow, when her husband took his truck to work, she would go out to the garage and clean out this car.

When she couldn't find the hymnal inside the car, she began to search the trunk. Although there were so many other objects in the trunk, she could not find that song book! She was beginning to get upset. She did not want to disappoint her pastor, but the book was not anywhere in the car. She would have to go and tell him.

As she approached the steps to the church, Pastor Stronghart's son, Ethan, came out the front door.

"Sister Sandra, are you okay?" he asked.

"I can't find the song book," she said, frustrated. "It is not in the car."

"Well, let's go back inside," he said, taking her arm.

He was such a little gentleman. She let him lead her into the sanctuary.

As they entered the building, she stopped, amazed. In just those few minutes while she was outside, the church had been transformed into the most beautiful place she had ever seen. Streamers had been draped across the backs of the pews and around the room, coming to a point above the front of the church. A trellis covered with roses – were they real? They looked and smelled real! – was at the front of the church, and her husband stood smiling at her, just in front of the trellis, with Pastor Stronghart beside him, and several men and women of the congregation standing in rows off to the sides. The room was filled with the fragrance of red roses. She stood near the door, trying to make sense of it all. Dr. Martin was sitting at the organ and he began to play, softly. She recognized the prelude to the wedding march, and all of a sudden, everything fell into place.

This was her wedding, her dream wedding! Ethan walked down the aisle and joined the line of men. Zooey followed him and stood beside her mother and the other women. Brother Jason appeared out of nowhere and was standing beside her.

"May I walk you down the aisle?" he said softly.

Sandra could feel herself grinning from ear to ear as the wedding march began. She took Brother Jason's arm and they walked slowly, as if in a dream, to her waiting husband at the front of the church. Everyone in the room was standing, smiling, looking at her. They all had known about this! They all must have helped decorate while she was outside, looking for that song book in the car. A wonderful feeling of love came over her as she looked into the eyes of her husband. He was smiling so lovingly at her as she was being brought to him. He had done all of this! He had gotten the idea to have a wedding, and he had planned it all, and what's more, he had kept it a secret from her!

As Brother Jason delivered her to her husband, she looped her arm in his arm as Brother Jason faded into the background. The spotlight was on her and Chester, and her eyes were glued to his. He had found something special for her birthday, for their anniversary, and she knew she would never forget this magical day as long as she lived. She was so happy, from the deepest depths inside of her. She did not want to cry!

"You may be seated," Pastor Stronghart instructed the congregation.

"Friends and loved ones, we are gathered here this afternoon to celebrate the joining of this couple in marriage. Yes, they were legally married thirty-five years ago on this date, on Sister Sandra's birthday, and today, they are renewing their wedding vows.

"God first made man, and when He looked at all creation, He said, 'It is good.' Then when He considered this man He had made, He said, 'It is not good for man to be alone.' God decided to make an help meet for man, and He took one of Adam's ribs and created woman. He did not create her from his head, to rule over him, or from his feet, to be trampled by him, but from his rib, to walk beside him; from his rib, which is close to his heart.

"God made one special woman for each man, and when you meet that one special person who is meant to be your other half, you know it in your heart. Chester knew from a young age – when he was just a child – that Sandra was the girl for him, and he never had to look anywhere else but right next door."

Sandra's heart was warmed every time she heard that, and today was no different. Now she felt warm all over her entire body. Was it getting hot in here?

"The union of husband and wife is one of the heart, mind, and body, and this union is intended by the Lord for their mutual joy, for the help and comfort given to one another in the times of prosperity and adversity. The union grows as the two people become one, in more and more ways, on a growing basis as their love for one another expands.

"Brother Chester and Sister Sandra, life is given to us as individuals, and the first lesson we must learn as a married couple is how to live together with each other. Love is given to us by our family and friends. We learn to love by being loved by others. Learning to love and learning to live together is one of life's greatest challenges. That is the goal of a married life.

"But the husband and wife should not confuse the love by worldly measures, for even if worldly success is found, only love can hold a marriage together. Mankind did not create love. God created love and He teaches it to us, and He gives it to us. He gave us the best love, when He gave us His Son, Jesus Christ.

"The measure of a true love is one given freely and that is freely accepted, just as God's love for us is given freely to us and unconditionally. Today is a glorious day that God has made, as you, Brother Chester and Sister Sandra, reaffirm your love and vows for each other. Both of you are blessed with God's greatest gift of all, an abiding and true love of each other, and the reward of a life-long companionship that entered your life through the love in your lives. As you continue to travel through this life together, remember it was love that got you here, it is love that will continue in your lives, and it is love that will cause this union to endure. I ask that you guard your heart and your love for one another, and hold that love for each other tightly in your hearts.

"First Corinthians, chapter thirteen, which is known as the 'love chapter,' tells us in the new King James version:

> *"Love suffers long and is kind;*
> *love does not envy;*
> *love does not parade itself, is not*
> *puffed up;*
> *does not behave rudely, does not seek*
> *its own, is not provoked, thinks no evil;*
> *does not rejoice in iniquity, but*
> *rejoices in the truth;*
> *bears all things, believes all things,*
> *hopes all things, endures all things.*
> *Love never fails.*

"Brother Chester, please take your wife's hands."

Chester took both of Sandra's hands in his, as they turned to face each other.

Pastor Stronghart continued. "Sister Sandra, will you continue to have Brother Chester as your husband and continue to live in this marriage? Do you reaffirm your love for him, and will you love him, keep him, and honor him in sickness and in health, and forsaking all others, be faithful to him as long as you both shall live?"

"I will," Sandra said, over the lump in her throat.

"Brother Chester, will you continue to have Sister Sandra as your wife and continue to live in this marriage? Do you reaffirm your love for her, and will you love her, keep her, and honor her in sickness and in health, and forsaking all others, be faithful to her as long as you both shall live?"

"I will and I do and I will!" Chester said enthusiastically.

"Ethan, do you have the rings?" Pastor Stronghart asked.

Ethan stepped forward and handed the rings to his dad.

Pastor Stronghart said a prayer of blessing over the givers and receivers of each of the rings. He then handed the rings to them.

"As the ring is a circle, without beginning or end, so is the love you have for each other."

Sandra looked at the ring in her hand, a brand new anniversary ring for her husband. Chester had done this, too!

"Brother Chester, will you place the ring on your wife's finger?" Pastor Stronghart asked, "and repeat after me: I give you this ring as a symbol of my vow, with all that I am and all that I have, I honor you, and with this ring I thee wed."

Chester put the ring on his wife's ring finger, and it clicked right into the ring she had been wearing since the day they had first gotten married, thirty-five years ago. "I give you this ring as a symbol of my love, with all that I am and all that I have, I honor you, and with this ring I thee wed."

Sandra looked at the ring her husband had placed on her finger. This was the ring she had told him she wanted ten years ago! He had remembered! She was really on cloud nine now.

"Sister Sandra, will you place the ring on your husband's finger?" Pastor Stronghart asked, "and repeat after me: I give you this ring as a symbol of my vow, with all that I am and all that I have, I honor you, and with this ring I thee wed."

She fumbled with the ring, almost dropped it, and tried to put it on Chester's ring finger. She could not get it over his knuckle! It didn't fit! Or, more likely, Chester's fingers were swollen, like they always were when he was nervous. He helped her push it onto his finger, and finally there it was, so beautiful and shiny on his rugged hand.

"What am I suppose to say now?" she asked. During her fumbling of the ring, she had forgotten what Pastor had just said!

The congregation laughed a little and Pastor Stronghart reminded her what she was to say: "I give you this ring as a symbol of my vow, with all that I am and all that I have, I honor you, and with this ring I thee wed."

"Chester, I give you this ring as a symbol of my vow and my love, with all that I am and all that I have, I honor you, and I love you and I thank God for you, and with this ring I thee wed," she said, looking into her husband's eyes, those eyes she knew and loved so well. He really did love her: she could see it and she could feel it, and today, he had truly shown to everyone his love he had for her.

Pastor Stronghart then gave the charge, putting one hand on each of their shoulders. "Brother Chester and Sister Sandra, as the two of you both now reaffirm your love for each other and the vows you made to each other many years ago, I charge that you each remember to cherish each other as special and unique individuals and that you each respect the thoughts and ideas of one another. And most of all, be able to forgive each other, and not hold grudges against one another. I charge that you live each day in love with each other, always being there to give love, comfort, and refuge to each, in good times and bad. I pray that God be with you, as He has been for the last thirty-five years, and fill you with His Spirit each and every day, as you grow closer to each other and closer to Him. Amen."

Pastor Stronghart turned to the congregation. "Since Brother Chester and Sister Sandra have now exchanged vows and rings, and they have pledged their love and faith for each other, it is my pleasure and honor to pronounce them husband and wife." He turned back to Brother Chester and Sister Sandra. "You may kiss your bride."

Chester swooped Sandra into his arms and gave her a big, romantic kiss, right in front of God and everyone. The congregation cheered and clapped.

Pastor Stronghart stepped aside as he said, "I am pleased to present to you, Mr. and Mrs. Chester Deacon."

Dr. Martin began playing the organ, and Chester escorted Sandra down the aisle. Sandra became aware that cameras were flashing all around them, from all over the church. As they were nearing the door, Chester stopped.

"What are you doing?" Sandra whispered.

Chester turned her around to face Pastor Stronghart as he made an announcement.

"The reception will be in the dining hall, so don't leave until you have something to eat!" Pastor Stronghart said loudly, over the buzzing of the crowd. "And also, Brother Chester and Sister Sandra, please come back to the front so we can take some pictures. Those of you who are in the wedding party, please stick around so you can be in the pictures, too."

Sandra really had to hold back the tears now. They did not have any pictures of their first wedding, and now, finally, she would get her wedding album! She was not a teen bride, like she had been the first time, but she was still a bride. She was a surprised bride! This day was getting better by the minute.

Chester led her back up to the altar as the crowd dispersed. Sister Stronghart, who was a professional photographer, set up her camera and a couple of lights on tripods.

"Does my hair look okay?" Sandra asked Chester.

"My beautiful bride, your hair looks perfect," he answered, wrapping an arm around her.

"Sister Stronghart, does my hair look okay for the pictures?" Sandra asked. "Chester is all goo-goo eyed and he can't see my flaws."

"Sister Sandra, your hair, your dress, everything looks

beautiful," Sister Stronghart said, as she adjusted the camera. "Let's start with a few pictures of just the two of you, then we will get the women, then we will get the men, then we will get everyone together."

"Sister Stronghart, you have to be in some of them," Sandra reminded her.

"When I get to that part, I'll set the timer," Sister Stronghart said.

When they finished taking pictures of every possible combination of the wedding party members, Chester began to lead Sandra back to the dining hall. People were sitting at tables, eating, and she could see that the members must have organized a potluck dinner.

As they turned the corner and stepped into the dining hall, she really could not believe her eyes. There, on a table in the middle of the room, was the most beautiful wedding cake she had ever seen, decorated in pink and blue, her favorite colors. It had five tiers, and it was absolutely lovely. She had not had a wedding cake before! After they had eloped, Chester had taken her to a diner to eat, and they had celebrated their marriage by sharing a piece of apple pie.

"We have just a few more pictures to take," Sister Stronghart said, bringing her camera into the kitchen.

"Everyone, can I have your attention, please?" Pastor Stronghart said loudly.

People stopped talking and only a few forks clanking against plates could be heard.

"The Bride and Groom are going to cut the cake," he said, and everyone turned to look at Sandra and Chester as they approached the table with the cake on it.

Sister Stronghart aimed her camera and Sister Evelyn handed Sandra a knife that had a white, lacy ribbon wrapped around the handle.

"How do we do this?" Chester asked.

Sandra had been to many weddings, but she had never paid attention to this detail.

"You both hold the knife and cut off a small piece and put it on that little plate," Sister Tammy said.

"And then you cut it in two smaller pieces, and you feed each other with it," Zooey added. "And be nice! Don't stuff it in each other's mouths."

Sandra and Chester were both laughing as they cut a piece of cake and each took part of it so they could feed each other. Chester was very nice and placed the little piece into her mouth, but she got a little more wild, and pushed the bigger piece in his mouth, getting frosting all around his lips and on his cheeks.

"Hey!" Chester said, wiping his face with a napkin. "I was nice!"

"And I was naughty," Sandra said, raising her eyebrows to him.

Everyone laughed.

Sandra thought, this had truly been the best day of her life. She had never expected that her husband could be so romantic, and on top of that, keep it all a secret from her! But he had, and she loved him so much for it. He really was the best husband any wife could ever have. She knew, without a doubt, that God had made them for each other.

## Jason

At almost four in the morning, Jason rode his bike around the back of the store to lock it in the employee bike cage. He was always energized after riding his bike to work, and he was excited about what the day might bring. Although it was still dark, he felt like he was glowing, because God was so good to him. He had found a house where several other young Christian men were living, and they needed another roommate. He was going to be able to rent a room and have a shared bath, kitchen and common room for only ninety-five dollars a month! That was truly a miracle that only God could have provided. Not only was it an amount he could afford, but he would be sharing a home with other Christian men, where they would share the household chores.

He knew it was time to move out from his mother's house. He loved her and he prayed daily that she would be delivered from her bad habits, but now he had to take care of himself. He had to get his own place and be responsible for himself.

He entered the building through the warehouse door, which was open. The truck must have arrived early this morning, so he got busy and got ready to start his shift. As the truck was unloaded, his job was to open crates and take the boxes to the proper area in the back room.

"Hey, Jesus Freak!" Ponton called. Ponton was in charge of the warehouse area, which meant he mostly just watched who went in and out of it.

"Good morning, Ponton," Jason replied. He did not

let the name-calling get to him. He had more important things to think about. He silently said a prayer for Ponton as he opened the first crate.

"You speaking in any foreign tongues lately?" Ponton asked with a laugh. "Abba-abba-blabba-blabba!" he yelled.

Jason ignored him as he continued to work. He had a lot of work to do and could not let himself get distracted.

"See any angels lately?" Erica, one of his co-workers asked, as she slid by him. "Oh, look, up in the corner, there's one!" she giggled. "Oh, wait, that's a spider. Ewww!"

"Good morning, Erica," he said politely, as he took the last box out of the crate. He looked around for a hand truck so he could put away these boxes.

"Oh, you ARE looking for angels!" she teased. "Look, there is one! Or, I could be one, if you want me to. Maybe I can come over to your house and show you how angelic I can be?"

"I don't think my mom would like that," Jason said, immediately mad at himself for being drawn into her conversation. He prayed that God would hold his tongue so he would not respond like that, but only be patient and polite.

"Oh, you still live with your MOM?" Erica asked, shouting it loudly so everyone in the warehouse could hear. "I thought you were a grown man, but I guess it's true what they say about Christians. Christians are just big babies, and you never can do anything on your own without asking Jesus – or your Mom!" She laughed wickedly. "How old are you, anyway? Fifteen?" She went into a fit of laughter, holding her side as she doubled over.

Jason did not respond to that comment. He loaded up the hand truck and began taking his load to the back room.

"Hey, look, if it isn't Holy Roller!" another co-worker, Andrew said, as he sat on a big box, eating a piece of beef jerky. "Have any revelations last night? Or are you going to put a curse on me because I didn't go to church this weekend? Are you going to send me to hell?"

"Good morning, Andrew," Jason said, as if Andrew had not just insulted him.

"Hey, Christian, turn the other cheek!" Mick said, as he mimicked slapping Jason on the face. Jason flinched, but didn't reply.

"So what happens when you run out of cheeks to turn?" Andrew asked.

"Well, I've got four I can turn to you," Jason snapped. He bit his tongue. He did not want to react like this! What would Jesus do in this situation? Well, He did call the religious rulers hypocrites and whited sepulchers, or bleached tombs. He was not always the gentle Jesus to everyone.

"Ooooohhh! That is bad!" Andrew said, laughing. "You are probably going to have to go to hell for that!"

Jason just smiled at him. Andrew's remark did not require an answer. The enemy was trying to rile him up, but the power of God was stronger than the power of the devil. Jason merely needed to yield to the Holy Spirit, in every situation. He again asked God for strength. The other thing he needed to do was to get some advice from his pastor. Pastor Stronghart had experience in just about every situation, and Jason knew he would have some helpful words to share.

## Patricia

Patricia looked around her apartment, satisfied. This was the kind of place to raise children. She had a little bit of furniture: two couches (that she had salvaged from the area near the garbage bin) and two old televisions (both had been given to her) in the living room, a dining room table with three mismatched chairs, and both bedrooms had a mattress on the floor for a bed. The walls did not have holes in them, and both doors, front and back, were able to be locked.

Her life had definitely improved since that day when she had taken her kids to church. She and her mother had repaired their relationship, and her mother had let them stay with her until Patricia could get back on her feet again. She had cleaned herself up – she had been clean for nearly four months now, without even one slip-up, and she finally was able to qualify for low-income housing. Now she had her own home and everything was falling into place.

Her mother had offered to watch Kandy, Lonny and Lesly while Patricia cleaned up her apartment. She could not remember the last time she had been alone, without the kids, but it had not been any time since she had become clean and sober. She was finished with the cleaning – she could take the dirty clothes to the Laundromat later – and she actually had some free time.

She went into the little living room and sat on one of the couches. She turned on one of the TVs and changed through the channels. She could get fourteen broadcast channels, and there was nothing good to watch. She had no telephone, so she couldn't call anyone, not one single book or magazine to read. For the first time in a very long time, she had nothing to do.

Patricia went to the kitchen and looked in the refrigerator. Not a thing was inside it, neither in the refrigerator or freezer, not a bottle of ketchup, a jar of mustard or a tray of ice - but that would soon change, when she received her food coupons.

She looked through the cupboards: a few mismatched cups and plates, and, finally, a half-full bag of pretzels. She grabbed the bag and began to eat frantically, trying to decide what to do with her time. She had at least two hours before her mother was expecting her to pick up the kids, so she could do whatever she wanted! But what did she have to do? Absolutely nothing!

She decided to go for a walk. Although they did not live in the nicest neighborhood in town, there was a small park nearby. She could go out to the park, get some fresh air, and then come back to her own home and take a nice, hot, leisurely shower before it was time to take the bus over to her mom's place.

She looked around through her scant belongings until she found the key to her apartment. She locked the door and started down the steps to the ground floor. As she turned the corner in the stairway, the door to the apartment below hers opened, and two young men, probably in their early twenties, stepped out, giggling, looking to the left and right suspiciously. She knew in an instant that they were high. She did not know them, but she had seen this type of behavior hundreds of times, if not thousands of times.

"Hey, guys," she said, trying to be friendly.

"Whoa! Where did she come from?" one guy asked, laughing.

"She came out of the sky," the other one answered, pointing a finger up toward the sky.

As Patricia approached the bottom step, the same apartment door opened again and another young man stuck his head out.

"Are you Star Child?" he asked her.

She laughed. "No, I am not Star Child," she said.

"Oh, well, I am waiting for Star Child to come," he said, scanning the parking lot with his eyes. "I don't really know what she looks like."

"Well, I can't help you there," she said, pausing at the bottom of the steps. "I do not know anyone by that name."

"I have seen you before," the young man said, examining her. "Are you related to Bob Smasherface, the adult clown?"

She laughed at the ridiculousness of the question. "No, I am not in any way related to any kind of clown," she answered.

"Because I thought I saw you at his family reunion last summer," he explained. "Not everyone there was dressed as a clown, you know. Some were dressed up, like, really fancy, making the clowns appear so much more prominent."

"No, it wasn't me," she said, getting ready to go on her walk.

"Well, do you want to party?" he asked. She could smell the remnants of burning drugs coming out of his apartment.

She stopped in her tracks. Oh, what sweet words she had been longing to hear, although she had been so strong lately, and staying as far as possible away from this type of situation. She had been so good for so long.

"So, come on in," he said, opening the door for her.

"I really shouldn't," she said, knowing that she really shouldn't.

"Do you have something better to do?" he asked, raising his eyebrows.

That was the problem, exactly. She had nothing better to do. She had been so straight for all this time. She deserved a little reward. She just needed a little bit, just for a little while, then she could go back to being straight. Oh, she needed this, so badly.

"Sure, why not?" she asked, as she followed him into his apartment.

Her mother's voice flashed through her mind: "Patty, are you making a wise choice?"

"Shut up!" Patricia shouted.

"Yeah, I knew you'd like it," the man said, grinning wickedly, as he welcomed her into his lair of evil.

## Carolina

"Come on, time to get ready for bed," Carolina said to her three grandchildren.

"Where is Mommy?" Kandy asked. "I want my mommy!"

Carolina was wondering that very same thing, but she did not want to let her anxiety show. Patty had left her children with her three days ago, saying she would return in the afternoon, and Carolina hadn't heard from Patty since she left them. Carolina was hoping and praying that there was a logical explanation, but she could think of no logical explanation, unless it had something to do with drugs.

"She will be back later," Carolina said hopefully. She had been doing a lot of hoping and praying for Patty these past few days. On the one hand, she was so happy to be spending time with her grandchildren, especially since she had been losing weight and was able to get around a lot better than she had when she had been so obese, but on the other hand, she was so worried about her daughter.

During the time when Patty and her children were living with Carolina, Patty had confessed that she had had a drug problem, but she had promised that she was over it, and she had been clean and sober for months. Patty had been going to church with her mother, she had confessed Jesus as her personal Savior, she had been baptized, and she had become stronger.

However, from the Bible studies lessons, which she had not been able to get Patty interested in, Carolina knew that the devil was a trickster, and that he targeted the weaknesses of Christians. Pastor Stronghart had been teaching in the Tuesday night Bible Studies class that the devil was a being who knew just exactly what kind of temptation each person was susceptible to, and that was the first thing he would try to use to draw a person away from God. He would never try to tempt Carolina with drugs, because that was not her weakness, but that was the kind of temptation he would use to draw Patty back into the life of sin she had been living before she had come to the church that day.

"I can't find my blankie," Lonny whined, helping Carolina to focus on her present situation.

"I think you left it in the bed," Carolina said, herding her grandchildren into the bedroom, the way a mother hen would gather her chicks into one area.

"Mommy?" Lesly asked, her eyes wide with question.

"She will come back later," Carolina said, as she tucked the three tiny children into one big bed.

"Grandma?" Kandy said. "I like spaghetti."

"Yes, so do I," Carolina answered, as she gave each child a kiss on the forehead.

"Maybe we can have spaghetti tomorrow. Night-night, Grandma," Kandy said, as Carolina turned out the lights.

"Good night, Kandy, good night, Lonny, good night, Lesly," Carolina said, pulling the door behind her. "I love you." She didn't close it all the way, because they were all three afraid of the dark.

She went into her kitchen and opened the refrigerator.

It was bulging with food, now that she had three more mouths in the house to feed, but she pulled out her Bible Studies lesson and got her Bible off the table so she could study. Although it was late in the evening, she needed a spiritual boost right now.

She settled into her chair with her Bible beside her and her lesson in front of her and she was really getting into the lesson when suddenly there was a pounding on her door. She prayed, 'please don't let it be the police, telling me bad news about Patty,' as she set aside her studies and got up to unlock and open the door.

There stood Patty, her hair a mess, all over her head, and wearing the same clothes she had been wearing three days ago.

"Hi, Mom!" she said loudly, with a big, goofy grin on her face. "I'm here for my kids. It's time to take them home."

Carolina glanced at the bedroom door. "Get in here," she said, ushering Patty inside her apartment and closing the door. "They are already in bed, asleep. Why don't you just cuddle up on the couch, and you can take them home in the morning? Or, better yet, we can all go to church together in the morning."

"Oh, no, I'm not tired," Patricia said. "I can take them home now."

"Do you have a ride?" Carolina asked, wondering if someone was waiting in the parking lot for them. "Because the buses aren't running any more. They stop running at eight o'clock on Saturday."

"Oh, no, I do not have a ride," Patty said, falling down

onto the couch. "Maybe I better take you up on that couch invitation."

Carolina was relieved. Patty was not acting like herself, and Carolina was afraid of what might happen if she tried to walk the kids home in the dark, especially since they were already in their pajamas, in bed and asleep. She glanced at Patty as she shuffled back to her chair and saw that she had already fallen asleep. Carolina turned to get a blanket and placed it gently over her daughter as she silently prayed for her, again.

## Jason

"Pastor, I know it's the devil against me, but he just won't let up," Jason said, as he helped Pastor Stronghart wash the windows of the church building.

"You have identified the enemy," Pastor Stronghart said, as he wiped a window, "so what weapon do you have to fight him?"

"The Bible says in Ephesians, 'after having done all, to stand.' I have been standing my ground and almost all of my co-workers keep taunting me, every time I go to work. I pray and I pray, but they won't stop. You would think they could find something else to do, someone else to bother." He took a squeegee and reached to the top of the window he was cleaning, and pulled it down to reveal a nice, clean, streak-free window.

"Is it getting to the point where they are bullying you, or discriminating against you because you are a Christian?" Pastor Stronghart asked.

"I don't know if I would call it bullying," Jason said, "but if I said some of the things they say to me to a gay person or a Jewish person or a person of another color, I probably would get fired. As Christians, we are not protected, even though they have that phrase about 'this organization does not discriminate on the basis of race, ethnicity, color, national origin, sex, disability, veteran status, political beliefs, religion, sexual orientation, or age.' Even the supervisors make fun of me."

"Just think about how many people made fun of Jesus," Pastor Stronghart said, "even when He was dying on the cross."

"I know, and I keep my mind on Him," Jason said. "It is the only way I can make it through the day at work. I know God gave me this job, I know He put me there for a reason, but do I have to go through these trials every day at work? Every single day?"

"Brother Jason, is this your dream job?" Pastor Stronghart asked, as he moved to the next window.

"No, of course it isn't," Jason said with a laugh. "I can't work in construction any more, so I just have to do what I can with my high school diploma."

"You have your high school diploma. Have you ever thought about going back to school?" Pastor Stronghart asked.

"What do you mean? Community college?" Jason had not really considered that possibility. He began to wonder what it might have to offer him.

"Or maybe technical school? You like computers, don't you?" Pastor Stronghart asked.

"I like them, and I think they have a million possibilities, but I don't even know how to use them," Jason responded, as he finished cleaning the window.

"I know one of the recruiters for the technical school, the one that is right downtown, and he has all the information about financial aid, and they even have a work-study program. I could give him a call. Or I can give you his card, and you can call him."

"You know, when I worked in construction, I sometimes saw the tech guys who would come in at a certain point and run the wires and set up the networks," Jason said, suddenly eager to explore the possibility.

"Maybe I could do something like that."

"I'll give you his card when we go inside. Why don't you give him a call? His name is Terry."

"Pastor, thank you. Every time I talk to you, God gives you the answers to give to me. I never even thought about it before, but I think I would like to go back to school."

"More education would certainly give you an advantage throughout your life," Pastor Stronghart said.

"I'm gonna do it!" Jason said. The problems he had at work would soon vanish, as he moved on to the next phase of his life. He could – and he would – get a much better job. God had just shown him the open door ahead of him.

## Patricia

Life was good for Patricia. She had found out the way to have the best of both worlds. She and her mother were on pretty good terms, she went to church once in a while so she could get her blessings, her new friends were always hanging out at her house, and her kids were happy. She did not find it necessary to be sober at all times, as long as she had her friends nearby, and she did not need to go to church all the time.

She got up from the couch to stretch her legs. Her new friends, Armond, Hammish, Marco and Kender were playing video games – this was why she needed two television sets, side-by-side, in her living room – and her kids were playing back in their bedroom. The rooms were thick with cigarette smoke, but nobody was doing drugs here today. She wandered back to the bathroom, looking in on her kids as she went by their room. They were sitting on their bed, that is to say, the mattress on the floor, and all the clothes her mother had bought for them were strewn around the room.

"Look at this room!" she shouted at them. "Pick up this mess!"

They looked at her in terror, as they gathered together at the far side of the mattress.

"You should take good care of your clothes and not have them all over the room!" she yelled.

They looked around the bare room, searching for a place to put the clothes. Patricia had not been able to find a free dresser for them, and she had not brought any hangers for the closet, since her children could not reach high enough to hang anything in there.

"Just pile them in the closet so they are not all over the room," she insisted, as she marched angrily to the bathroom. They could be so ungrateful sometimes. They did not even care anything about their clothes.

When she finished in the bathroom, she wandered through the kitchen to find something, anything, to eat or drink. She grabbed the bag of potato chips that was on top of the refrigerator, then she opened the refrigerator door to see what was inside. Three cases of beer were neatly stacked on the racks, but there was nothing else. Well, a beer sounded good right now. It would really compliment the chips, so she pulled out a can and returned to the living room. She lit another cigarette and squeezed onto the couch beside Kender, to watch another round of racing on one TV and zombie-killing on the other TV.

Yes, life was very good these days. She had everything she needed.

## Lorenzo

"Lorenzo!" Conya screeched. "Lorenzo! Did you get the milk at the store that I told you to get this morning? Your baby needs it! Don't you care about her? You know I can't go anywhere at this time of the month! I am in PAIN!"

Lorenzo was nearly fed up with Conya, even though he had promised himself that he would not let her get on his nerves. He had been tempted so many times to just walk away and never come back, or to get in with that crowd who promised easy money, but since he had been involved with the church and going to services regularly, he was learning to be patient, and to have respect for people who did not have respect for him, like his loved ones. Conya was just yelling at him because she didn't feel good. That was no reason for him to snap back at her. He wanted to respond with kindness, with love, with understanding.

"Yes, my darling," he called, with an exaggerated compassion. "I picked up two gallons when I went out earlier."

"Two gallons of milk? What are we going to do with two gallons of milk? Ebony will only drink about half a gallon, and all the rest will go bad!"

"Mommy, please don't yell at Daddy," Ebony pleaded. Lorenzo knew she would be sitting by her mother's bed, taking care of her mother's every need while she was 'in the manner of women.' Conya had been having bad cramps every month, so painful that she was confined to bed for two or three days per month. Lorenzo let Ebony sit in the bedroom with Conya, so she wouldn't be lonesome, and he tried to stay out of her way until she was feeling better.

"It won't go to waste," Lorenzo said, coming to the bedroom door. "I'll drink some of it."

"When did you start drinking milk?" Conya asked, as if he had started drinking rum or some other sinful drink.

"I like milk," he said simply, not wanting to remind her that he had always been drinking milk.

"Well, don't be drinking all of Ebony's milk," Conya insisted.

"I won't," he promised.

"You better not!" she shouted. She was so irritable, she could get in an argument about anything.

The phone rang. He was saved by the bell as he dashed to answer it.

"If it's Mama, I don't want to talk to her!" Conya yelled.

"Good afternoon," Lorenzo said calmly into the receiver.

"Is this Lorenzo Williamson?" the voice on the other end asked.

"Yes, this is Lorenzo," he answered.

"Who is it?" Conya shouted from the bedroom.

Lorenzo ignored her as he tried to hear what the woman on the phone was saying.

"Hi Lorenzo, this is Katy Parker from Tri-City Transit,

and we have reviewed your application and your interview scores and your test scores, and we would like to make you an offer."

"I'll take it!" he exclaimed, silently thanking God.

"I haven't told you yet what it is," Katy Parker said.

"Okay, that's good, I'm listening," he said, holding himself to the floor so he would not start jumping up and down.

"Who is on the phone?" Conya yelled at him.

"We have one full-time opening for a driver coming up next month, and we would like to get you in next week for a training with the driver who is retiring before he leaves. Are you available next week?"

"Oh, yes, I am!" he said, clenching his fist and shaking it with excitement.

"We will be starting you off at eighteen dollars an hour, plus benefits," Katy Parker told him.

"That sounds perfect," he answered, thinking of how much more that was than his unemployment compensation, which was scheduled to run out in two weeks. Oh, God was so good! He was always right on time!

"We will see you, then, on Tuesday morning at seven o'clock," Katy Parker said. "You can come to the personnel office when you arrive, and be sure to bring your CDL license and your social security number with you."

"Thank you, Ms. Parker," he said.

"You have a nice day, Lorenzo," she said, and she hung up the phone.

"Yaaaaa-hoooo!" Lorenzo shouted. "I got the job! I got the job! I got it, Baby!" he yelled, as he danced into the bedroom.

"You got a job?" Conya asked, as if she didn't believe him. "You finally got a job? Doing what?"

"Driving for Tri-City Transit!" he shouted, unable to keep his voice down. "I start next week, on Tuesday."

"When do you start?" Conya asked, typically not listening to him.

"I start next week, on Tuesday," he said, moving close to her.

"So you are going to go off and leave me alone all day long, every day?" Conya asked, pouting. She leaned back in the bed and stared at the ceiling.

"Baby, this is the break I have been waiting for, what I studied and worked for, why I got my CDL license," he explained, gently stroking her hair.

"So, when do you get your first paycheck?" she asked, turning her gaze to the ceiling.

"I don't know the exact date, but it will be just about the time my unemployment checks run out," he said, adding, "so that is like a miracle in itself. Isn't it great? God is so good. He might not come when you want Him, but He is always right on time!" He began to do a little dance around the room.

"Yeah, Baby, I guess that is a miracle," Conya said. "When we go to church, we will have something to thank God for."

"Why wait until we go to church?" Lorenzo asked.

"We can start thanking Him right now!"

He raised his hands in the air and started to shout, as he skipped around the room with joy and praise.

## Officer Shotgun

He had no other choice: Ted Shotgun would have to go to that church during a Sunday service and find out exactly what was going on. His schedule had become so crazy, he had not had a chance to get there any time during the past few months. Now he had a Sunday morning off. He could infiltrate the congregation and see for himself, from the inside, what kind of racket that preacher had going.

He had put on a nice pair of slacks and a dress shirt, although he had chosen to not wear a tie, and he pulled his car into the parking lot. He was certain that some of the lawbreakers in the church would recognize him as a police officer, but he was not going to announce it. He was going to observe and take notes. Maybe he could even record some of the criminal activity using his phone. He was ready for anything.

When he entered the building, at least ten minutes before the morning service was scheduled to start, he was surprised to see people already operating like they were involved in rituals. A few people were kneeling up front at the altar, praying, and a man was playing the organ while another man was playing the drums. Ted slipped into a pew unnoticed and tried to make himself invisible. He remembered why he hated churches: all this phony acting, the pious platitudes, the bragging ceremonies. This show of dramatic religion was making him very angry.

A young man came up to him and shook his hand, welcoming him to the church. Ted smiled courteously, apprehensively watching this man, wondering what his scam was. A lady then came up to him and also shook his hand, saying some nonsense about being glad he had come to worship with them today. He smiled, thinking how she had intentionally tried to throw him off the track by using the word 'worship.'

A few more people came into the church, and that preacher – the same one who had been on TV – stepped into the pulpit. Ted was watching for any activity that would indicate something illegal was going on, but they were doing a good job of covering it up. He would have to put on his sneaky eyes, to be able to see what was going on beneath the surface. He wasn't stupid. He had his illegal-activity radar going at full capacity.

The entire group of people started acting foolish when the preacher told them to praise the Lord. Suddenly he knew what was going on here! That preacher had them hypnotized! He would say something and everybody would start shouting and clapping and jumping up and down. This was not a regular church service. These people were under some kind of a spell. He probably kept them drugged so he could control them, like cult leaders were known to do.

When it came time for the offering, they did not just pass the plate around through the pews like they would do in a normal church, but everyone walked up or even danced up to the front and put their money in a large basket while the man played the organ joyfully. Ted avoided this ritual, taking note of this suspicious activity. Why were they acting so happy to be giving their money to a worthless cause? One didn't have to be an accountant to know that these few people and their little offering could not pay the bills at this building. Even in this part of town where the rent might be low, they still had to pay for electricity and water.

Ted saw people passing things secretly to each other, and slipping things into their mouths, and he knew it had to be drugs, by the reaction of the crowd to everything the preacher was saying. They were acting like they were over-excited, yelling and screaming at every phrase. Everyone in the room was behaving irrationally, shouting and waving their hands. Nobody was just sitting in his seat and listening, like they were supposed to be doing in church. These were obviously all drug addicts who were high, and they even had children in here. Yes, he knew what was going on here, and he was going to put a stop to it. He could get Children's Services involved, and he would shut down this operation, no matter what he had to do.

When the preacher began to say it was time for the 'Word from the Lord,' Ted knew it was time for him to leave. This whole thing was a farce, a center for nonsense. He had collected enough evidence. He slipped out of the building while everyone was closing their eyes, pretending to be praying.

## Sandra

Sandra awakened much earlier than usual this morning. She wasn't feeling well – was it heartburn or was she just full from last evening's dinner? It was only three-thirty in the morning, and she didn't have to get up until four-thirty to make Chester's breakfast and lunch, but she couldn't go back to sleep. She tried to get comfortable, and as her new anniversary band brushed against her pillow, she was again reminded of the wonderful husband she had, and the wonderful anniversary surprise he had given her. She would have to think of something extra special to make him for his birthday, which was coming up next month.

She turned over to snuggle into her husband's arms, the safe place she had been every night for more than thirty-five years. She was just starting to get comfortable and relax, finally, when the alarm sounded. Sandra always got up a few minutes before Chester, so she could start breakfast and have it ready by the time he got out of the shower. Even though she was not feeling very well, she pushed herself, knowing she could lie back down as soon as Chester left for work. She could clean up the kitchen later.

She pulled herself out of bed, swallowing hard to try to get rid of that clogged feeling in her chest, and put on her robe over her pajamas.

"Good morning, my dear," Chester mumbled, still half asleep.

"Good morning, Chester, my love," she responded, as

she tried to take a deep breath. She felt like she couldn't get any fresh air in her lungs. She pressed on.

As she was walking through the living room to the kitchen, she suddenly knew she could not make it without resting. She was so very tired, and she could not take a deep breath. She stepped sideways to go to the couch, recalling her beautiful wedding, and the room went black.

## Pastor Stronghart

The phone rang at 4:47 on Thursday morning. Pastor Stronghart was already in his home office, studying the Bible and making notes for his sermon on Sunday. He reached for the phone on the first ring, so as not to bother his family, who still had a couple of hours to sleep before they had to get up.

"This is the day the Lord has made," he said joyfully.

"Pastor, my wife just passed away," Brother Chester said, with a sob in his voice.

"Brother Chester? Did you call 9-1-1?" Pastor Stronghart asked, standing, as he reached for his jacket.

"Yes, and then I called you," Brother Chester said.

"I am on my way," Pastor Stronghart said. He ran up the steps to his wife's side.

"Is everything okay?" Shannon asked sleepily, rolling over to look at him.

"Brother Chester just called and said his wife just passed away," Pastor Stronghart said, as he placed his hand gently on his wife's forehead. "I'm going over there now."

"Do you want me to go with you?" she asked, starting to get out of bed.

"No, I am on my way right now. I'll call you." He touched her cheek.

"Poor Brother Chester," Shannon said.

"But at least we know where she is," Pastor Stronghart said, "safe and sound, in the arms of Jesus."

"Drive carefully," Shannon said, leaning up to give her husband a kiss.

He leaned down to meet her lips. "I'll call you later," he said, as he rushed out the door.

At this time of the morning, there was almost no traffic, and Pastor Stronghart made it to Brother Chester's house in a few minutes. He was surprised to see the emergency vehicles had not arrived yet. He parked down the street to leave room for the emergency team and ran to the Deacons' front porch.

Brother Chester was waiting for him at the door and let him in.

"She is right over there," he said, pointing across the room. Pastor Stronghart could tell he was trying not to cry.

Sister Sandra was in her bathrobe, lying on the floor near the couch. She looked so peaceful, like she was sleeping, with a slight smile on her face. Pastor Stronghart went over to her to feel for a pulse on her neck. She felt cool, and he knew she was gone from this world.

"I was just getting out of bed," Brother Chester explained, "and I heard this big thump, so I called to my wife to see if everything was okay. She didn't answer me, so I rushed in here, and there she was, just like that. I thought maybe she passed out, so I sat down and put her head on my lap. She didn't move and she didn't respond, and so I got up and called 9-1-1. Then I knew she wasn't going to wake up and I called you."

The sound of sirens filled the air as they drew close to the house.

"Did you try to do CPR on her?" Pastor Stronghart asked.

"I don't know how to do it," Brother Chester cried.

"How long was it before you called me?" Pastor Stronghart asked, calculating the amount of time since Brother Chester had called him. He had just rolled Sister Sandra's lifeless body onto her back and was about to start CPR when the emergency team arrived at the door. Pastor Stronghart stepped back and let the team do their work.

"My wife didn't want to be revived," Brother Chester said softly, as they were connecting wires and equipment to her body. "She wrote it down on her medical directives."

The team tried to revive her anyway, but it was no use. She was gone.

Pastor Stronghart took Brother Chester aside and put his arm around him.

"She is in a better place," Brother Chester said, looking at his wife's body.

"She would not want to come back here, even if she could," Pastor Stronghart reassured him. "She is there with Jesus now."

"Pastor, there's something we never told you," Brother Chester said, his voice cracking. "We told you we could never have children, but we did. We had a baby boy when she was just twenty years old, when I was in the army, and the baby came too soon, and he died before I got to see him. I couldn't get home in time.

"We already had his named picked out. We named him Darren. She was in the hospital and she held him for a few hours before Jesus came and got him. We couldn't have any more children after that." He stopped to sob a couple of times. "Now she is there, in heaven, with our baby Darren. She finally gets to hold him again."

Pastor Stronghart put both arms around Brother Chester to comfort him as the emergency team collected their equipment.

"I am sorry, Mr. Deacon," one of the medics said. "We did all we can do. She is dead. Do you want us to take her in the ambulance to the hospital?"

"What for?" Brother Chester asked, pulling away from his pastor. "She isn't going to wake up. Pastor, what do I do now?"

"Brother Chester, it's time to call the funeral home."

Chester sat down on the couch and began to weep.

"Which one do you want to use?" Pastor Stronghart asked. "I can call them."

"I don't know, you pick one," Brother Chester said, attempting to clear his throat. "Pastor, I have to tell you something before you call them. I have life insurance through my job. We always thought I was going to go first, and I have a pretty good policy. But we never bought life insurance for my wife. We don't have anything in savings. We just never imagined that she would go first. How am I going to pay for her funeral and her burial and everything?"

"We will work something out," Pastor Stronghart assured him, going to the phone.

"She wasn't even fifty-four years old," Chester said, putting his head in his hands.

"And now she is with Jesus," Pastor Stronghart said. He put the phone back on the table and went over to sit beside Brother Chester. There was no hurry to call the coroner. Sister Sandra's status was not going to change. They could wait a few minutes.

"She is in heaven, and she is waiting for you to join her," Pastor Stronghart said. "Remember, as Christians, we have hope. When our loved ones die, we are not without hope like people who do not have Jesus. The apostle Paul tells us in First Thessalonians 4:13, 'But I would not have you to be ignorant, brethren, concerning them which are asleep, that ye sorrow not, even as others which have no hope.' When he says, 'concerning them which are asleep,' Paul is referring to the death of the body. This never refers to the soul or the spirit of man, because the spirit of man does not die. The spirit returns to the presence of God. Even the Old Testament teaches this. In Ecclesiastes 12:7 we read, 'Then shall the dust return to the earth as it was: and the spirit shall return unto God who gave it.' Your wife is asleep in Jesus."

Brother Chester nodded his head. Pastor Stronghart was aware that these words were probably just passing through his mind, but he continued to give him encouragement.

"What is death? Death is separation. It is not the ending of the person's spirit or of the person's personality. These do not die. When you die, the real 'you' goes on to be with the Lord if you are a child of God. It is the body that disintegrates. Death is a separation of the body from the individual, from the person. The body disintegrates, decays, and decomposes. 'Dust to dust and ashes to ashes' applies only to the body.

"The spirit and the soul do not die. In Second Corinthians 5:8, Paul says that to be absent from the body is to be present with the Lord."

"She is absent from that body and she is present with the Lord," Brother Chester said, slowly nodding his head. He looked over at his wife's body. "She does look like she is just sleeping."

"She closed her eyes on this side, and when she opened them, she was in heaven," his pastor said.

Chester stood up and went to kneel by his wife's body. "Save a place for me, my darling," he said. "I'll see you when I get there."

## Patricia

Things were not going well for Patricia. She had thought she could handle everything herself, but now she knew her mother was right, again, and as usual. She needed some help. She had lost her apartment and she and her kids were staying in the homeless shelter for women and children, but they were on their last day there. Her time had run out and she had not followed all the guidelines. She was going to have to take her kids back to her mother's place, and her mother would only welcome them if Patricia promised to start going back to church again.

Had it just been a coincidence that things started going well at the same time she started going to church? Or had God really been blessing her? Right after she made a commitment to go to church, she and her mother had made up, she had been accepted for the low-income housing program, and she had been able to kick her habit. They had moved into a pretty nice apartment and they had stability for a few months. When she stopped going to church, one by one, things were taken away from her, like God was punishing her for leaving church.

She would have to start going to church again. She had to let God get her life back in order, because she had really messed it up. She fell to her knees and asked God to help her, to direct her. She had to do it for her kids, if not for herself. She cried out to Him, telling everything that was in her heart. She felt He was listening to her, and He was giving her another chance. She wasn't going to mess it up this time. She felt as if this might be her last chance, but she couldn't do it by herself. She knew she needed God's help. She had to let Him help her.

Patricia went to the main desk and asked to use the phone, saying it was an emergency, which it was. She dialed her mother's number.

"Mom?" she cried. "I really messed up and I need your help, and I need God's help. I want to go back to church, and me and the kids need a place to stay for a little while."

"Patty," her mother said firmly, "there is something we need to do. We need to help our pastor. Where are you? I'll come and get you, and I'll tell you all about it."

# NOW

Shannon walked ahead of her husband and the police officer, dreading each step as it brought her closer to the back door of the church. The wind was biting and the air was nippy. A shiver made her entire body shudder as she fumbled for her keys. Her hands felt fat and slow, not wanting to open the door, reluctant to show the inside of the building.

In the darkness, she struggled to see which key fit the back door lock. She silently cursed the city for not replacing the light bulb in the streetlight.

"Come on, get that door open," the officer growled, "and I mean, NOW."

She finally forced the key into the lock, lifted and twisted while holding the door knob, the only way to get the key to turn in its rusty old mechanism. The door was damp and heavy on its hinges, protesting as she pulled on it.

The inside of the building was not any warmer than the outside, but at least she couldn't feel the wind in here. Her mind was spinning as she was shivering. What was he expecting to find here? The church was in a poor neighborhood and the church building had nothing of value to the outside world. She switched on the light in the kitchen and turned to face the two men.

"This is it, *Pastor*," the officer sneered, leaning into her husband. "Your jig is up."

"Seriously, Officer Shotgun, I don't know why we are

here," her husband said. He was not even shivering. She wondered, how could he not be cold in this frigid building and damp weather?

"Because you are going to show me exactly what goes on in that room over there," the officer said, pointing with his nose. "Something is going on here, and I am going to find out what it is. Come on, both of you."

He slightly shoved her husband, who, in turn, bumped against her.

"Excuse me, my dear," he said quietly, into her ear.

"No whispering!" Officer Shotgun shouted. "Get moving. You are not going to get out of this one."

She walked beside her husband with the officer close behind them. As they stepped out of the kitchen and into the hall, she could see a light coming from under the door to one of the classrooms, the largest classroom. She looked at her husband with a question mark on her face. He saw it too, but he just shrugged as they kept walking toward the room. Something *was* going on in that room… but what?

"Right in here," the officer said, giving them a little push toward the door.

Her husband reached for the door, and although he usually would hold the door for her as she went through first, this time he held up his hand to stop her, and he paused before entering the room.

"Get moving," Officer Shotgun barked.

As she followed her husband into the room she was confused. A group of people, some she knew from church, others she had never seen before, were in the room, sitting at the student desks, facing toward the front of the room. What were they doing here now? Were they having a class? She looked to see what they were looking at, but no one was at the front of the room, until the officer directed her and her husband to go up there, as the officer followed closely behind them.

She saw Sister Carolina, Brother Chester, Sister Evelyn, Sister Patricia and her children, Brother William, Brother Jason, Brother Lorenzo, Pastor Fields and his wife, Sister Tammy. She didn't know the others in the room. Her mind was racing, trying to figure out what was going on. She quickly stopped herself from imagining the worst. She was afraid to say anything, so she just waited.

"Okay, *Pastor*," Officer Shotgun said, "why don't you tell me why all these people are gathered here tonight, on a stormy night like this?"

"It looks like they are gathered here for a class or something," her husband said, "but, actually, I don't know. Why don't you ask them? I didn't even know they were here until we came in, just now."

"Yeah, right. Where's the stuff?" Officer Shotgun asked, looking around the room suspiciously.

"I'll tell you all about the stuff," Brother Jason said boldly, standing to his feet. "Pastor Stronghart gave me the confidence and a reference so I could get a job, and then he helped me get enrolled in the technical school so I can make a better life for myself."

"Pastor Stronghart helped to save my house," Brother William said, as he stood and lifted his head high. "He encouraged me when I was hopeless, and he introduced me to a man who helped me with my legal battles. I would be homeless right now if it weren't for my pastor."

"He saved our marriage," a man said, one who was holding a woman's hands in both of his hands. They stood up together. "He gave us free counseling when we didn't have any money and we were just about to call it quits. He gave us insight that could only come from God, and that gave us what we needed to get our marriage back on track. And here we are, still together."

"This pastor right here, Pastor Stronghart, helped me when my wife died," Brother Chester said, pulling himself to his feet, choking up a little while speaking. "He even did my wife's funeral for free. Pastor, I am still going to pay you for that, when I get caught up on all those bills."

Sister Carolina cleared her throat and struggled to get to her feet. "Pastor Stronghart helped me get on track to lose weight," she said. "If it hadn't been for him helping me, I would not even fit in this little desk." She slapped her palm on the desk for emphasis. "And also, he helped me say good-bye to my dad, when I wrote a letter to him, since I didn't have the chance to talk to him before he died."

"I will have you know," Brother Lorenzo said while standing to his feet, "Pastor Stronghart stuck by me when I didn't have a job. For almost a year, I was looking for a job and I never thought I was going to get one. He kept encouraging me, and he helped me get my CDL license. Then I still couldn't find a job, but he did NOT give up on me! I was ready to go back over to the old neighborhood and start dealing drugs, do anything for money, but he kept being that positive force, and he stuck by me until I finally got a job! And it is a good-paying job, one I never would have tried for, because if it wasn't for Pastor Stronghart, I never would have thought I could get a great job like that."

"Speaking of drugs," Sister Patricia said, motioning for her children to stand with her, "Pastor Stronghart helped me get off drugs. I was a drug addict, and I had lost my home, and I was about to lose my children – these three children right here – and I had lost all of my self-respect. But Pastor Stronghart had faith in me and he kept praying for me and pointing me in the right direction, even when I did not want to go that way. I fell away a couple of times, but every time I came back, he welcomed me. He always treated me with respect, he never stopped praying for me, and he and God finally got me off drugs for good."

"Pastor Stronghart pulled me out of the depths of depression," Sister Evelyn said, also standing. "When my daughter went off to college, I didn't even know I was depressed, but I missed her so much. Really, my life was missing something, and that something was the Word of God. Once Pastor Stronghart got me on a Bible studies plan, my depression lifted and I was given a new life."

"Pastor Stronghart gave me a chance to be in the ministry," Pastor Fields said, standing near his seat. "At first, I didn't have a degree, and he helped me get into divinity school. I struggled, but he kept praying with me and keeping me on the right track. When I graduated, he ordained me. He opened this ministry to me, to let me become an associate pastor here."

Another man Shannon didn't know stood up and cleared his throat. "My name is Cyrus. I have never been to this church before. When I was in the hospital dying of cancer," he said quietly, "this pastor came and prayed for me. The doctors had given up on me, but Pastor Stronghart let me know that God never gives up on us. The doctors had told me I had a very slim chance of surviving, but here I am, fully recovered, thanks to this man praying to God with me and for me. He gave me hope when I had no hope, and he didn't even know me. By the miracle of God, I stand before you tonight fully recovered."

The room was quiet as everyone looked at Cyrus.

"He saved my life," a man in the back of the room said, a well-dressed man, the final person in the room to stand. All eyes turned to him.

Shannon didn't know this man. She glanced at her husband, and from his expression, she figured, he didn't know him either.

"My name is Harold Trumbuck," the man said. "Pastor Stronghart, I have never actually met you, but you did save my life. I often thought about coming here to thank you, or to call and thank you, but I never did. One evening, I was sitting on the edge of my bed with a gun in my hand. I was about to kill myself. My problems were overwhelming and I was about to end it all.

"Then, because the room was so quiet, I turned on the TV, and there you were. It was like you were looking right at me. You said, 'You might feel like life is not worth living. You might be contemplating suicide.' I knew God was using you to talk directly to me.

"You told me that God had great plans for my life. I prayed with you that day, and now I am the vice president of the company where I work. That day, I was about to kill myself because I hadn't gotten a promotion. You saved my life, and when the guy who did get the promotion left the company a year later, I got his job, and not long after that, I was promoted to vice president. Pastor Stronghart saved my life and because of that, I got the promotion at work that I deserved. Thank you, Pastor Stronghart."

Everyone in the room was now standing and they all began saying, "Thank you, Pastor."

Shannon could not hold back the tears, for the love of God that was flowing in this room was tremendous.

Her husband turned to Officer Shotgun, who was leaning against the wall with his mouth hanging open.

"Officer, I guess you are right," Pastor Stronghart said humbly. "Something IS going on here."

## ALSO AVAILABLE FROM EVERLASTING PUBLISHING

### Novels by Dana Pride
- » *The Hidden City (Book 2 in Devastation Trilogy)*
- » *So How is THAT a Bully?*
- » *After the Great Devastation (Book 1)*
- » *The Red Cloak*
- » *Nightmares of Murder*
- » *No One Like You*
- » *Existing*
- » *All These Things*
- » *Kissing a Dead Man*

### Non-fiction books by Dana Pride
- » *How to Get Fat Without Even Trying*
- » *What Really Happened in Mexico*

### Poetry books by Joseph Fram
- » *Joseph's Journey, Volume 1*
- » *Joseph's Journey, Volume 2*
- » *Joseph's Journey, Volume 3*
- » *Joseph's Journey, Volume 4*
- » *Joseph's Journey, Volume 5*
- » *Joseph's Journey, Volume 6*
- » *Joseph's Journey, Volume 7*
- » *Joseph's Journey, Volume 8*

### Other titles available:
- » *Coptales by Steven Martin*
- » *Moses' Chisel by Steven Martin*
- » *Nathan is Nathan, by Jahla*
- » *Nathan Art: Autistic-Artistic by Nathan*

*Now also available to download as e-books!*

*http://everlastingpublishing.org*

*http://danabooks.8k.com*

*Everlasting Publishing*
*PO Box 1061*
*Yakima, Washington 98907*
*USA*